TEMPTATION

Shadows of the Heart
Book One

I0520200

Sandy Sullivan

Erotic Romance

Erotic Romance

Temptation
Copyright © 2017 Sandy Sullivan
Print ISBN: 978-1-944122-36-2

First E-book Publication: August 2017
First Print Publication: February 2018

Cover design by Dawné Dominique
Edited by Ariana Gaynor
Proofread by Maranda Melton
All cover art and logo copyright © 2017 by Sandy Sullivan

Dedication

This book is dedicated to all of you who love cowboys. For me, they are the ultimate hero. They personify everything I love about a man and I hope they are special to you as well. Enjoy the new series!

Temptation
Shadows of the Heart
Book One

Sandy Sullivan

Chapter One

Gravel crunched under the car's tires as Charlie Abrams drove down the single lane, overgrown driveway toward the huge barn in the distance. Yellow pasture grass swayed in the breeze blowing across the ground, pushing the long stalks back and forth. Excitement skittered down her spine, causing goosebumps to rise on her arms as she took it all in.

The warmth of the day beat down on the car, heating the inside enough she needed the windows down to cool it.

The sweet dry scent of hay permeated the air.

Gray three-rail ranch fencing lined the drive, leading her toward her destination. *I'll need to paint that.*

When she finally reached the end of her journey, she shut the engine off and sat staring at the large red structure before her.

She giggled as she pushed open the car door and stepped out. Her boots making a grinding sound on the rocks, and a warm breeze picked up the ends of her long brown hair, whipping them around her shoulders before letting the flyaway strands settle again.

She could feel the smile on her face as she glanced to her right. Her steps took her toward the gate that separated her from the largest of the pastures. The rusty latch gave with a little effort on her part as she pushed against it, barely able to open the metal barrier.

With a happy sigh, she took several tentative paces through the long grass, letting it brush against the palms of her hands as she moved. Wildflowers bloomed everywhere. It was like a massive splash of color on a canvas with the blue skies above, the waves of grass, and the hundreds of flowers.

A hearty laugh escaped her lips as she twirled around in circles for a moment, with her arms open wide, and a joyful heart.

It's all mine!

She couldn't believe she'd actually made her dream come true, well at least part of it. A ranch of her own and a family to raise had been something she'd worked for all her life. The family would come in time, she figured, but for now, she had the ranch.

As far as the eye could see belonged to her lock, stock, and barrel. True, it needed work, and lots of it.

A deep voice came from near the fence. "Uh, can I help you?"

She spun around to come face to face with the most gorgeous man she'd ever seen. Saliva pooled in her mouth before it went completely dry.

Hard muscles stretched as the man used the shirt in his hands to wipe the sweat from his chest. Worn jeans covered him from hip to feet, molding enticingly to his hips and legs as her scrutiny wandered further south. Dusty boots peeked out from under the hem of his pants.

"Ma'am?"

Her gaze snapped back to his face. Dark eyes stared at her from beneath a straw cowboy hat. A little smirk lifted the corners of his mouth as he cleared his throat and one eyebrow lifted over his right eye.

"Is there somethin' I can help you with?"

She licked her suddenly dry lips. Her voice came out in a little squeak. "Uh, sorry."

"Are ya lost?"

"Oh, no. Actually, no I'm not lost." She took a couple of steps in his direction, the rusty gate separating them until she pulled it open. "I just got here."

A full on, blinding smile met her gaze, stopping her heart in her chest before it slammed against her ribs as it restarted.

"Well now. Who might you be?"

"Charlene. Charlene Abrams." She held out her hand.

"Abrams?" He took her palm in his.

"Yes." The feeling enveloping her as she held onto his hand made her stomach flip over. Butterflies danced low in her belly. Not liking the feeling, she slowly pulled her hand from his grasp.

"I see." He frowned.

"Something wrong?"

"I was expectin' a Charlie Abrams."

"You were?"

"Yep." He took off his hat, giving her a beautiful view of his brown, thick hair before he slipped his shirt on and replaced his hat on his head. "You wouldn't be his wife, would ya?"

"No." She laughed slightly as she looked down at the fancy pointed toe boots on her feet. "I'm Charlie."

"Huh?"

"My real name is Charlene, but my friends call me Charlie."

"Well now. This could cause a pickle if I ever saw one."

"I don't understand."

"Let me introduce myself. I'm Caleb Armstrong. I believe you hired me to be your foreman."

"Oh." Her gaze met his again as she realized what he said. "Oh!"

A white dog with multiple spots, gray fur in several areas, and a brown muzzle raced up beside the man and promptly dropped into a sitting position as it nuzzled Caleb's hand. The dog eyed her and gave a low growl. "Easy boy." He glanced back up, catching her gaze with his. "I'm sorry. This is kinda awkward."

"No, it's fine. I should have told you when I'd be here. I should have called or something."

The wind whipped her hair off her shoulders, making her grab it in her hand and hold it to the side of her neck.

"I didn't realize I would be workin' for a woman."

"Is that going to be a problem, Mr. Armstrong?"

"Might be, Ms. Abrams. You see, I'm not used to workin' for a woman. Women don't own ranches in these parts without a man around to carry the heavy load, do the ground work, and handle the men workin' for them."

"That's what I hired you for."

"I get that, I really do, but we aren't married. There's a difference between a foreman and the man of the house."

She took a step closer. "I don't need a man of the house." With both hands on her hips and her hair a tangled mess from floating around her, she said, "I left one of those in Washington when I got in my car and headed down to Texas."

"So there is a Mr. Abrams?"

"No, there is not. Abrams is my maiden name. I took it back when I finalized my divorce after finding my husband in bed with my best friend." Her throat felt raw. Her eyes itched from unshed tears. She'd cried most of the way to Texas without anyone seeing or hearing her, as she blasted country music. Done with men and done with tears, she'd dried her tears on the outskirts of Shadow, Texas and drove on until she'd come to her dirt road, the one leading to *her* ranch.

The moment her divorce had been final, she'd taken her settlement, bought the property, and made her plans. Raising and training horses had been her dream since she'd been a little girl. Now, she planned to make that dream a reality and she'd be damned if any *man* was going to stand in her way, sexy or not. "Listen, Mr. Armstrong. If you have a problem—"

He pushed his hat back on his head. "I didn't mean to piss you off. Things are done a certain way around here. A woman doesn't run a ranch."

"Well, I guess I will be the first in the area then. If you are going to help me, then fine, you are welcome to stay. If not, I suggest you get off my property." She stomped past him on the way to the house sitting about five hundred yards from the barn. A shiver rolled through her as the scent of sweaty male hit her like a brick and she fought the urge to glance back over her shoulder. *Damn him!*

The gray wood steps creaked as she stepped on the bottom one. The weathered front door had a large window in the top half with a white gauzy curtain covering it.

The keys jingled in her hand when she pulled them from her pocket and slipped one into the old lock. The tumblers scraped as she turned the key.

Footsteps crunching on gravel behind her made her turn around to find Caleb standing at the bottom of the stairs. "I'm sorry, ma'am. You caught me off guard so I probably said some things I shouldn't have." He removed his hat and held it between his large hands.

When he glanced up and caught her gaze with his, her ears began to burn with embarrassment to be caught ogling him like she was. He was a mighty fine looking man. Standing at probably six feet of hard muscle and trim hips, she couldn't help but notice him even if she didn't want to. A man was the last thing she needed in her life. They were a necessary evil to get the job done, but she'd be damned if she would let her libido get in the way of making her dreams come true, especially with the hired help.

"Mr. Armstrong—

"Caleb, please." His lips lifted in a grin, showing off his straight, white teeth.

She swallowed past the lump clogging her throat, not sure if being on first name basis with this man would be a good idea. "Caleb. I accept your apology. Are you willing to help me build this into the best damn cutting horse ranch in the area?"

"Is that what you want?"

"Yes."

"Do you know anything about cutting horses?" He took the two steps up toward her.

She backed up so her shoulder blades hit the side of the house.

Space between her and this disturbing man would be a good idea. He was her employee after all. "Yes. My father was a championship rider and trainer."

"Charlie Abrams is your father?"

"Yeah. I am named after him, well sort of." She swallowed as he moved a step closer. "I never rode cutting horses in competition, but I've been around horses my entire life, well most of it except during my marriage. My ex-husband didn't do animals. I have trained some myself. Not professionally, of course."

"Didn't do animals, huh?"

"Not at all."

"Where did you live in Washington?"

"Seattle. He worked for Microsoft." His eyes twinkled with mirth. He was laughing at her, which pissed her off even more. "I need to get my things into the house, so if you will excuse me."

"Of course. I still have some work to do in the barn to get ready for your horses." He shoved his hat back onto his head. "When does the first shipment arrive?"

"The stallion will be delivered the end of the week. The mares won't be here until the end of the month."

"Good. We have some time to get him settled in then before all hell breaks loose." He stepped down to the gravel at the bottom of the steps before turning back toward her. "Do you have some other men coming to work the place?"

"No. I was hoping you would help me hire some men from around here."

"That might be a bit difficult."

"Why?"

"They will work for me, but they won't work for you." He tipped his hat and headed back toward the barn.

Her gaze followed his trek across the yard, his dirty boots kicking up dust. She couldn't help but notice his ass in those jeans, fitting his tight little butt like they were molded there by a lover's hand.

She cleared her throat and brought her attention back to the bottom of the steps where his dog sat staring up at her. "What?"

A shrill whistle whipped the dogs' head around toward the barn before he took off running to where Caleb had disappeared through the large double doors.

The quick exhale of breath brought her thoughts back to the tasks at hand. She had a hell of a lot of work to do to get the place up and running before the first horses arrived.

* * * *

Caleb walked inside the barn and headed straight for the tack room. He needed a cold drink, a cold shower, a stiff whiskey, or a woman. He shut the door behind him, took a seat in the rickety old wooden chair sitting in front of the desk on the wall, and tipped back on the two rear legs. What the hell was he going to do? This whole situation seemed like a clusterfuck.

He rubbed his fingers along the scruff growing on his jawline. "Damn it to hell." The legs hit the dirt, almost breaking from the weight. "I thought this was going to be an awesome gig working for some city-slicker who thought raising cutting horses was an easy way to make a buck. How in the hell am I supposed to make this work? That gal ain't no pushover if she's Charlie Abrams daughter." Never mind she was hotter than a firecracker on the Fourth of July.

Tall, slender, built like a brick shithouse, and with lips made for kissing. It was going to be hell keeping this strictly business. The moment he'd laid eyes on her spinning in the middle of the pasture with her arms out giggling like crazy, his dick had been standing up and taking notice of every curve she had. Long brown hair primed for twisting a fist in and eyes the color of the sky meant she was major territory for any red-blooded man in the area. *I have definitely been without a woman far too long.*

A digital clock sat on the desk amongst the papers waiting for him to review. The red numbers only read three in the afternoon. Too early to quit for the day, but damned if he didn't want to bag it right now and head to the Riverside Watering Hole and get a beer. Those papers wouldn't finish themselves, unfortunately.

Why did this have to turn into a problem? His life seemed to always take these detours, nothing ever worked out for him. He'd barely finished high school, not being one of those smart kids. He'd worked hard all the way through, trying desperately to keep a roof over his head as well as his mother and his brother, since his dad was on the road all the time when he was little. He didn't have the grades to go to college, but he did have a way with animals, horses mostly. Training them came naturally to him.

He had his own issues and babysitting some woman who thought she could run a ranch even if her dad was a world champion was the last thing he needed.

Maybe he should give her the benefit of the doubt and see how things went. He didn't have anywhere else to be right now anyway. She had paid for his salary in advance to get him to her place to help her set up. It was the least he could do, he supposed.

His dog nudged his hand, drawing his attention down as he absently stroked the dog's head. His buddy. His constant companion. He'd found the pup in a ditch on the side of the road one winter, cold, wet, and hungry. The dog had attached himself to Caleb the moment he'd lifted him into the cab of his truck and taken him home. He couldn't ask for a better sidekick. Sparky was a mutt, but Caleb knew he was some kind of Australian Shepherd or Healer because of his quickness and willingness to herd. That dog had turned into the best thing to happen to him in a long time.

The pedigree of the stallion she had arriving in a few days, sat to his left on top of the pile of papers, drawing his attention.

A soft whistled of appreciation escaped his mouth when he picked it up and scanned the document. The horse had one hell of a family tree. His Sire was a champion even he recognized and his Dam had one hell of a lineage as well. If he was as good as his papers looked, he'd be a fantastic addition to her stable. He had to give her credit. She obviously knew her horseflesh.

He knew by the emails they'd exchanged that she had some mares with some great backgrounds as well, but she wasn't just going to breed them. Her plan was to train some quarter horses as cutting horses too. He thumbed through more of the papers, looking over each one and separating them into piles by breed and sex.

The work was piling up as he checked out the stock arriving soon. He would need help and quick, but where to find it was another question he needed to answer. Hands in town would be reluctant to work for a woman in any capacity, never mind he'd be the one in charge. First things first though. He needed to find some top trainers to get this operation running as soon as the stock arrived. Training a cutting horse wasn't easy and it took time, not something he was sure they had. Normally to get the best horse up to speed to get top dollar from an enthusiast, you needed twelve months or so. If you trained for just the basics, it took three to six months. He knew a few good trainers, but it would take time to convince them they needed to be part of this operation. Not an easy task by any means.

To convince his *boss* of what they needed to do would take some quick thinking. He wasn't sure Ms. Abrams would be easy to steer in the right direction.

A knock sounded on the tack room door. He knew he was the only one on the place besides Charlie. "Come in."

The door creaked open with a noise loud enough to get your back up. *I need to oil that.*

"Mr. Armstrong?"

"Caleb, remember?"

"Uh, okay. Caleb. I wanted to apologize for earlier." She pushed the door open further and took a step inside. Her gaze shifted quickly around the room before coming back to him. "I know you are here to help me and I need you."

Need was a pretty strong word right at the moment, and one he wasn't sure he wanted to explore beyond what he *needed.* "You hired me to do a job. I'm willin' to do what I can to make this work for you." He pushed to his feet, realizing she was kind of short compared to his six foot five frame. "You have to trust me to do what I think is best for the operation."

"I do or I wouldn't have hired you."

"Good. I have a few people I know who might come to work here, but it's going to take money. They won't do it without a good wage."

"I understand, but I've also made some phone calls or should I say a call to my father."

"Oh?"

"Yes. He gave me some names as well."

"If we both work on this, then we should be able to get some good help, but I have final say on who is hired."

"No."

"No?"

She shook her head as she placed her palms flat on the desk. "We can talk about who you want to hire. I'll go with that, but I have the last word on who comes to work for me."

Damn, stubborn woman. "Fine," he gritted out between his teeth. After all, she was the *boss.* He pushed his hat back on his head and sighed.

"Things will work out. I'm confident we can do this." She took a step back and turned on her heel. "I'll let you know what I find out."

He didn't respond, preferring to let his temper cool a bit before he blew his stack. It wouldn't be a good idea to go off on her right now.

A drink sounded better and better.

With a quick glance at the clock again, he decided to get a little more work done in the barn before he called it a night. It was only about ninety minutes before quitting time, giving him just enough to get one more stall cleaned out before he could leave.

The radio in the barn played George Straight as he grabbed the square tipped shovel and the yellow wheelbarrow. The big stall on the end would be a good place for the stallion when he got here. It would give him plenty of room and was secure enough he wouldn't be able to get loose.

The half-door on the stall opened easily under his hand allowing him to swing it open and secure it to the wall.

Shit lined the enclosure from one side to the other, telling him someone hadn't cleaned it for a long time. The wooden handle of the shovel was smooth on his palms, the weight itself familiar and soothing. There was nothing like cleaning out stalls to take your mind off anything you were contemplating and right now, he was contemplating how little Miss Charlie's mouth would feel under his. Nothing that he would ever find out, but damn he sure wished he could.

He needed to forget that right now. She wasn't what he needed. Nope. No siree. A woman like her would be way too much work on his part. Someone who didn't have her sights set on a huge undertaking such as building up this place would be a much better idea.

The whole place had been run down from what he could tell. Not to the point where Charlie would be better to tear it down and build new, but enough that repairs would be required like a new roof, fresh paint, and new boards in some of the stalls. There was a nice enclosed arena behind the barn where she could show what the horses could do to potential customers.

He wasn't sure about the house, having not been inside. It could use a nice coat of paint as well and the yard would need some work. Overall, it wasn't a bad place although he had no idea what she paid for it.

It had been on the market for some time before she'd purchased it, the former owners had fallen on hard times and lost the place to the bank.

For now, the best thing he could do would be to clean up this stall, find somewhere to get a cold beer, and hook up with a willing woman to ease the ache in his balls that started right about the time one pretty little dark-haired filly had shown up.

Yep, sounded like a good plan to him.

Chapter Two

Country music reached her ears loud enough she had a difficult time hearing the bouncer at the door asking for her identification. "What?"

He got near her ear. "ID?"

"Oh." She reached into her purse and pulled out her driver's license before handing it to him.

He glanced it over, looked at her, and then handed it back. With a tip of his hat, he moved onto the next person behind her.

Wow. The Riverside Watering Hole was hopping. Of course, it was Friday night and it appeared to be the place to be this evening in Shadow, Texas.

She let her gaze roam from one side of the place to the other, taking in the atmosphere. Cowboys lined the bar, resting their booted feet on the rail underneath. Hats in several colors as well as different materials graced their heads. Women in jeans and western shirts moved between the men, smiling and flirting. Boots were on everyone's feet, tapping to the beat of the music, two-stepping around the dance floor, or taking a load off.

Someone bumped into her from behind. "I'm sorry, ma'am. I didn't see you."

When she turned to face the voice, she was surprised to see a pretty young lady with long blonde hair pulled back in a ponytail, caring a tray with about ten bottles of beer. "No problem."

"There's a seat at the end of the bar if you are looking for one. It's pretty busy tonight, so not many to choose from."

"Thank you."

"Sure."

The girl disappeared into the crowd toward the back of the bar, the sea of cowboy hats parting for her, then coming back together to close up the hole like she was never there. Charlie shook her head and walked down the small space left between those standing around talking and the others leaning on the bar.

Not sure why she decided to come here tonight, especially by herself, she figured she'd drink a beer and then go home. She had a lot of work to do on the house to clear the years of dust and dirt clinging to everything. Her bedroom and the kitchen were clean, but that was as far as she'd gotten today after she'd left Caleb in the barn.

Speaking of the good-looking cowboy, she knew she would have her hands full with him. He definitely had the personality of someone used to being in charge and taking orders from someone else would be difficulty at best.

Charlie found the empty barstool and slip up on it. She recognized a George Straight song the band played. They weren't too bad, but they certainly weren't in the league with the King of Country Music.

The bartender thumped his knuckle on the bar, drawing her attention. "What are you havin'?"

"Bud, please. In a bottle if you have it."

"Sure thing. Comin' right up."

He disappeared down the bar to her right for a few minutes as she turned on her stool to check out the people near her. She'd always loved to people watch and this crowd was amazing. The bar itself was pretty fantastic too. Very rustic with wood floors scuffed from years of boots on it, peanut shells were everywhere underfoot, making her wonder why they would do that. Beer signs graced the walls in several spots, blinking on and off with their neon vibrancy. The restrooms were near the back in the corner, sectioned off from the rest of the chairs and tables by a wooden wall with different cattle brands burned into the surface.

"Here you go." The bartender set the bottle down on a napkin behind her. "Three fifty."

When she spun back around, she took notice of the man. He had a friendly face with round cheeks, a barrel chest, and a nicely trimmed beard that covered his jaw line. Blue eyes the color of sapphires twinkled with mirth as he leaned in.

"Thank you," she said as she pushed a five toward him. "Keep the change."

"Mighty kind of you." He didn't leave right away, just kept staring at her for a moment. "You're new here."

"Yes." She brought the bottle to her lips and took a nice long drink. "I bought a place outside of town."

"Oh yeah?"

"Yes."

"Which one?"

"I believe it used to be called Thunder Bow?"

"I know that place. The Cheslers' use to own it."

"That's what I understand."

"You bought it, huh?"

"Yes sir."

"What are you plannin' on doin' with it?"

"I'm going to be raising, selling, and training cutting horses." She took another sip of her beer. "I have a foreman working for me, but I need to find some trainers. Do you know anyone who trains cutting horses that might be looking for a job?"

He rubbed his hand along his jaw as he gazed over her shoulder. When she followed his line of sight, she noticed the blonde-haired waitress serving a table behind her. "I might, but I'll have to ask around."

Not sure if he was thinking of the waitress or someone else, she said. "If you know of someone, have them come out to the ranch. I would love to talk to them."

"I surely will, ma'am."

She held out her hand. "Charlene Abrams."

"Nice to meet you, Charlene. Folks call me Jack."

"Nice to meet you as well." She held up the beer. "And thank you for the beer."

"You're welcome."

When he went back to serving his other customers, she watched him from her peripheral vision. He seemed very nice and he probably knew a lot of people in the area. It would be a good idea to keep in touch with the very friendly bartender. He could probably tell her about many of the folks in town.

After she took another long draw from her beer bottle, she turned on her stool as she rested the bottle on her thigh. It had been so long since she'd been out with a man dancing, dining, or whatever, she'd almost forgotten how fun it could be.

Her marriage to her ex had gone south so quickly after their wedding, she'd almost began to wonder if her best friend and maid of honor had been screwing her soon to be husband before the ceremony. She'd never really paid that much attention to how close they were until after she'd found them in bed together. The pieces had fallen into place when she'd come home early from work one afternoon, catching them in the act. In her bed, no less. She'd been hurt and furious, but after she'd walked out with her suitcases in hand, she'd realized all along that something strange had been going on there and that her husband had only married her for the Abrams name and her father's endorsement in the rodeo circles.

Now, she didn't care what the asshole did or whom.

"Hey, baby."

She glanced to her right, noticing a tall, blond cowboy with more rhinestones on his ass and shoulders than most of the women in the room. Growing up around the rodeo circuit, she'd seen a few cowboys in her day, and this was not one of them. To be polite, nodded before bringing her bottle to her lips.

"Wanna dance?"

"No thank you. I'm here with someone."

"I've been watching you. You came in alone and I haven't seen you talking to anyone but the bartender."

"I'm not interested, so back off."

"What a bitch."

"You don't know the half of it, buddy."

He took her beer bottle from her hand and poured it down the front of her blouse. "You probably need to go home now, little girl, and leave the playing to those of us who know what we want."

The cold liquid made her inhale sharply as it dribbled down between her boobs, soaking the front of her shirt. She jumped to her feet, pulling the wet material away from her front. "You son of a bitch!"

He began to laugh as he took a step back.

A red haze clouded her vision as she tried to get her anger under control. For too many years she'd had to put up with this type of behavior of cowboys on the circuit when she'd traveled with her dad. They all thought if she didn't sleep with them that she was whoring around with any guy but him.

Deciding she wasn't going to put up with the man's behavior and she would make it known throughout the town she wasn't a push over, she got right up in his face, grinning like a Cheshire cat, and kneed him in the balls.

The fool folded like an accordion into a pile of moaning man flesh as the crowd around them backed up.

"Anyone else want to be stupid?" she asked, holding out her hand.

One cowboy stepped forward, but as her anger dissipated, she realized it was Caleb. "You okay?" he asked bringing his lip close to her ear.

His scent was musk, male, and some kind of really sexy cologne. Goose bumps rose on her arms as his breath tickled the skin of her neck.

"Yeah." She pulled the wet fabric away from her front. "Just wet." She shook her head and sighed. "I guess my night is over."

"Do you need a ride?"

"No. I have my car here."

"I'll walk you out."

"Not necessary, but thank you." She pulled her car keys from her front pocket. "I guess I'll see you tomorrow."

"No, it's Friday. I won't be there until Monday since there aren't any animals to care for."

She nodded, realizing he would probably party all weekend and drag his ass into bed early Monday morning for a few hours of shuteye before work at sunrise. "True. The work that needs to be done right now is maintenance stuff and cleanup."

"If you need help with stuff on the house, let me know."

"I'm fine for now. It's basic cleaning." She nodded as she stepped to the left. "Good night, Caleb."

"Night, Charlie."

She glanced over her shoulder when she reached the door, only to catch him smiling at a woman who had her back to the wall. He had his arm over her head as he leaned in close and put his lips near her ear. Charlie wondered if the woman reacted to him the same way she had. Surely it was a normal reaction to a good-looking guy. His smile probably made women all over town sigh.

Realizing it was going to be a long, lonely night, she pushed open the outside door of the bar, welcoming the cooler air as it hit her in the face. The last thing she needed right now was a roughneck cowboy. Her life was on the right track and she planned on keeping it that way.

Thirty minutes later, she pulled down the gravel driveway of her new home. She'd left the light on in the living room and on the porch so she could see where she was going being unfamiliar with the house.

She stopped her car near the front and turned off the engine as she stared at the house. When she'd seen the pictures of the old house, she'd fallen in love with it. It needed some TLC, but that wouldn't be a problem as far as she was concerned.

A long wrap-around porch graced the front and sides with huge picture windows on either side of the door. She planned to put some rocking chairs with a little table between them on the front porch so she could sit and watch the sunset while sipping lemonade.

The plans she had for the house were things she would do over time to bring the beautiful old house back to its farmhouse glory.

She pushed the car door open and stepped out before shutting it behind her and walking toward the porch. The steps creaked a little under her weight as she walked up the wooden planks to the entryway and opened the door.

When she closed the panel behind her, she stopped to listen to the silence. It was kind of eerie being by herself. She laughed a little as she walked into the kitchen and put her keys on the countertop near the coffee maker.

With two fingers, she held out the material near her chest. The scent of beer hit her like a brick. "Wow. I really need a shower."

She worked to strip off her blouse, undoing each button down the front as she walked down the hall to the bathroom.

The room was one of her favorites in the house. It had been decked out in black and white by the former owners, with white subway tile halfway up the walls and black accent tile along the upper border. There was a huge claw foot tub in the corner big enough she could submerge her whole body in it without even trying. A large walk in shower stall stood in the corner, totally enclosed in glass with alternating white and black subway tile clear to the top. What she loved the best was the huge rain shower head. She could stand in there for hours letting the hot water cascade over her shoulders and back, washing away the day's labor.

The glass opened with a tug on the handle and she turned on the shower, adjusting the water to the right temperature.

After she got her jeans, boots, socks, blouse, and bra off, she stepped into the enclosure, pulling the door shut behind her before sliding under the spray.

Water cascaded over her in long rivulets while she tipped her head forward, letting everything wash down the drain from the day. All the stress of meeting Caleb and realizing he would be a force to be reckoned with, dealing with the asshole at the bar, understanding how hard it would be to get the ranch to her liking, and then talking with her father, who in his infinite wisdom made her feel like a child, all came down to this. Nothing mattered at the moment. Everything would work out in time and she just had to believe that her plans would come to fruition with a lot of hard work, a little luck, and some damn good horseflesh. It all began with that.

The stallion would be here by the end of the week. His pedigree was impeccable from what she'd seen and he would make some mighty fine offspring. The pictures didn't do him justice. The moment she'd laid hands on the magnificent animal, she'd been intrigued. He was gorgeous and had fantastic conformation, but the thing that struck her was how gentle he was. Stallions were notorious for being difficult. Not this one. The moment she'd stepped into the showing area, he'd taken right to her, allowing her to stroke him before nuzzling her arm for more petting.

The water began to cool, making her realize how long she'd been standing there daydreaming. After she quickly washed her hair and body, she shut the water off and grabbed a towel hanging over the shower enclosure.

Soft, warm, fuzzy material cushioned her feet as she stepped out. The bath rug was the one luxury she bought herself when she moved in. There was nothing like that softness wrapping around her toes.

She hummed to herself as she opened the door and walked into her bedroom. The décor complimented her style. The big king sized bed was way too big for just her, but she loved having the room to spread out. The long dresser along the back wall was ornate with its scrolling woodwork and carved front with the huge mirror above.

A large cowhide rug graced the floor, tickling the bottom of her feet as she retrieved her pajamas.

Bed sounded so good right now. Drifting off to the sounds outside would be the best thing she could think of.

Crickets sang in the distance, frogs croaked, bringing the answering sound from another nearby.

Once she had her pajamas on, she glanced out the window into the pasture beyond. Fireflies danced on the warm, moist air.

A light flicked on in the barn, startling her, until she saw the outline of a man in the doorway. Not sure if she should check it out or not, she slipped her feet into her blue Eeyore slippers and pulled open her door. The floorboards creaked under her weight as she made her way toward the front of the house.

Maybe I should call Caleb.

Terror gripped her like a tight band around her chest, squeezing until she felt lightheaded. Someone was on her property and she had nothing to protect herself, much less anyone who would care.

I need to call 911.

She found her phone sitting next to her keys on the kitchen counter. Grabbing it in her hand, she held it tightly as she crept toward the door trying to decide if she should dial the sheriff or check it out herself first. *Don't be an idiot!*

The clock in the hall struck midnight. No one should be on her property this time of night. Caleb had said he wouldn't be back until Monday, so who in the hell was in her barn?

An old baseball bat stood like a sentinel in the corner by the door. She didn't own a baseball bat. She sent up a silent prayer to whoever was watching over her as she grabbed it in her shaking hands and slowly pulled open the front door.

This was not the way she wanted her first week in her new home to end, but she'd be damned if she wouldn't defend her property.

Silently she crept out the door and down the front steps, making her way to where the light shone brightly in the middle of the walkway of her barn. The bat held high, she moved closer and closer until she could see someone moving from one stall to another as if he was looking for something.

Taking a deep breath, she yelled, "I have a gun and I'm not afraid to shoot you. The police are on the way, so come out with your hands up." She felt brave and invincible right at the moment while she contemplated what to do from here. Hiding behind the big barn door, she could see movement in the stall before the man stepped out into the light.

"Easy, darlin'."

What the hell?

Chapter Three

"Caleb, what in the hell are you doing here? You said you wouldn't be back until Monday, and I almost hurt you."

"Can you put that down, please?" he asked, nodding toward the weapon in her hand.

"Oh, sorry." She lowered the bat to her side as his gaze swept over her from head to toe before bringing her arms over her chest to hide her reaction to his perusal.

A grin appeared on his lips. "I didn't mean to scare you."

Her breath hitched. "Well, you did. I couldn't figure out who would be in my barn at midnight."

He stepped closer as he lowered his hands from where he'd held them up. "I hadn't planned on coming back out here, but after the incident at the bar, I wanted to make sure you got home all right. Since I was already here and wide awake, I figured I'd get a little work done."

"I didn't even hear you drive up."

"My truck is pretty quiet." His grin widened as he looked down at her feet. "Nice slippers."

After she glanced down, her gaze met his again as she shrugged her shoulders. "I was getting ready for bed."

His grin slipped a bit. "I didn't mean to disturb you."

"It tends to do that when someone is flipping lights on in my barn in the middle of the night when I didn't expect anyone to be here but me."

He nodded toward the bat. "I thought you said you had a gun?"

"I figured whoever was out here would be more willing to show themselves if I said I had one."

"Do you?"

"Have a gun?" When he nodded, she answered, "No."

"Get one, but make sure you know how to use it."

"I don't think—"

"Listen, Charlie, this can be a rough place especially for a woman alone. Get a gun. Learn how to shoot it if you don't already know, and keep it by your side." He swept past her, headed for the doorway. When she turned to follow his progress, he said, "Now that I know you're home safe, I'll go on home." He stopped right before moving out of the light of the barn and tipped his hat. "Sweet dreams. I'll see you on Monday."

She stood on the threshold watching him get into his truck, flip on the headlights, and then disappear down the driveway until she couldn't see the red glow of taillights anymore.

With a heavy sigh, she flipped off the lights in the barn and made her way back across the lawn toward the house.

Nights like this, she really hated being single and alone.

The moment she was back in the house, she locked the deadbolt on the door, set the bat next to the casing, and headed for the kitchen. After her run in with the gorgeous Caleb, she needed a drink and the bottle of red wine chilling in her refrigerator sounded really good right then.

* * * *

A loud pounding woke her the next morning, her head splitting like someone was driving a nail right between her eyes.

"Holy shit." A groan escaped her lips as she rolled off the couch and hit her knees. She glanced around realizing she must have fallen asleep in the living room.

The empty bottle of red wine sat next to the equally empty glass.

Someone yelled from the other side of the front door.

"Just a minute!"

She forced herself to her feet, glancing down at the rumpled pajamas she had on, the one Eeyore slipper still on her foot, and wondered what the hell had happened. The only thing she remembered was coming in from the barn after Caleb left, grabbing the wine, and sitting down to watch late night television. Now the sun was up and someone was pounding on her door.

A quick swipe of her hands over her hair and a run of her finger over her fuzzy teeth, she peeked through the hole in the door to see the waitress from the bar the night before, standing on her porch.

"Uh, just a moment, please." She glanced at the clock on the wall, squinting to bring the numbers into focus. "Crap. It's ten o'clock?"

She cracked the door open until she could see the girl. "Can I help you?"

"Ma'am? Jack Porter from the bar told me to come out to see you about a job?"

"I'm sorry, but I overslept this morning. Why don't you have a seat on the porch and I'll be out in about ten minutes."

"Um, okay. I can come back if you want."

"No, no. It's fine. Just hang tight. I'd like to talk to you."

She ran down the hall to her bedroom, throwing on a pair of jeans, a t-shirt, and her boots before darting into the bathroom to quickly brush her teeth and run a brush through her tangled mass of hair. A ponytail holder to pull back her hair and she was as ready as she'd ever be.

When she opened the door a few moments later, the girl climbed to her feet from where she'd sat down on the steps.

"Hi. Again, I guess."

"Hello."

The girl held out her hand. "My name is Amy Montrose. Jack Porter from the bar said you were looking for trainers."

"I am. I am planning to train, raise, and sell cutting horses. Have you trained horses before?"

"Yes, ma'am. My daddy owns a farm outside of town, but it's hard for a woman to make it in the business, if you know what I mean."

"I certainly do." Charlie had a good feeling about Amy. "My father was a champion in the cutting horse competitions for years, but when I talked to him about training them, he steered me away from it, even tried to get me to go into nursing or something more feminine. My heart is in the horse business though."

"I know exactly what you mean. I've always wanted to train."

"I do have a foreman working for me who will be overseeing the training and caring for the animals. I will be doing most of the sales myself."

"That's fine, ma'am."

"It's Charlene, but my friends call me Charlie. I hope you will do the same."

"Sure."

"My stallion arrives the end of the week with the mares coming a little later. I do have a couple of horses coming in from people who need them trained, which we will do as well. I will need to see you in action, but I'll give you the benefit of the doubt. I'm assuming you don't have a lot of references for your training abilities."

"I have a few. People around here who I have worked for, but you're right, not a lot."

"No problem. I'm sure you will be able to prove your worth." She started down the steps of the house. "Come on. I'll show the barn and training facilities. Luckily the people who owned this before were into showing animals at one time. There is a fabulous arena already built in the back and there is a fantastic training area where we can bring in some cattle for you to work with."

Amy followed close on her heels. "Who is your foreman?"

"Caleb Armstrong." The girl stopped for a second and Charlie glanced back. "Is there a problem?"

"No. I guess not." Amy started walking again although her steps seemed a little more measured now that she was in step with Charlie.

When they reached the barn, Charlie flipped on the light illuminating the walkway. "The stalls are in here. The stallion will be kept near the back so there isn't any accidental insemination, but all the mares will be of high quality. I want to make sure that I control the breeding times and which mares are being bred." They moved further down until they came to a door. "Through here is the training arena." The door creaked under her hand as she pushed it open until it banged against the wall on the other side. "As you can see, it is well equipped and very functional."

"This is awesome."

Amy moved passed her, her eyes wide as she glanced around.

"There will be several trainers employed here when we are up and running at full speed, but for now, there will only be a couple."

"Will there be living quarters here?"

"In the future, yes. For now, there are not. Is that a problem?"

"No, ma'am. I live with my parents now, so I can drive over when my shift starts." Amy's attention came back to her. "I'd be pleased to work for you, Charlie."

"I'm glad to have you onboard then. When can you start?"

"Two weeks be okay? I need to tell the bar I'll be leavin'."

"That's fine." They closed the door behind them as they moved back into the main part of the barn. "Pay days will be bi-weekly and we can discuss your rate when you do the paperwork for employment which will be on your first day. Rest assured, it will be a fair wage."

Amy nodded as they walked back through the big barn doors. "I will see you in two weeks then."

"Great. Welcome to Abrams Cutting Horses."

They shook hands before Amy headed for her truck.

How would Caleb take having a woman trainer? Well, it didn't matter because he answered to her, right?

* * * *

Monday morning dawned bright and early as Caleb drove down the road toward Charlie's place. Birds chirped loudly as he stopped the truck near the barn.

Today would be the start of something good, he decided. He had some minor work to do on the barn before the stallion arrived, but he was excited to see the animal after looking over his pedigree.

When he stepped out he could hear the radio inside playing a great country song. He smiled as he shut the door and made his way through the double doors. Someone whistling along with the song drew him down the dirt walkway until he stopped outside one of the stalls and found Charlie scraping and shoveling shit from the floor into a wheelbarrow next to her.

He liked the sight. "Hey."

She spun around, a startled look on her face as she pressed her hand to her chest. "God, you scared me."

"Sorry. I didn't expect to find you out here."

"I can shovel with the best."

"I see that."

She scraped a few more shovelfuls before she stopped to take a sip of water from the bottle hanging out of the pocket of her overalls. She looked damn cute with the straps of those overalls over her shoulders and the tank top beneath. Her hair was pulled back in a ponytail, but it still hung down to almost her waist. She had a baseball cap on her head, but it did little to keep her hair out of her face. "Wow. I don't remember this being so hard."

"You are probably out of practice."

"Yeah, you could say that. It's been about five years since I cleaned stalls." She took another sip from the bottle.

His gaze went straight to her graceful neck as she swallowed. A drop dribbled down her chin, taking a path down her neck before it disappeared in the edge of her top. *Shit!* He needed to get it together, otherwise she'd know exactly how sexy he thought she was and how much he wanted to see how she'd react to his kiss.

Her lips were wet and shiny as she swiped her tongue across the surface. "How was your weekend?"

"What?" His thoughts were not on her words, but how the overalls fit over her breasts and how that tank top did nothing to hide the upper swell from his view.

She smiled. "Your weekend?"

"Oh, it was fine. After I left here the other night, I went home, drank a beer, and went to bed." He leaned against the stall door. "Nothing exciting. What about you since you were all dressed for bed?" He'd taken the time to go out to her place under the ruse of doing some work, at midnight, but really he wanted to make sure she'd made it home all right. After the idiot at the bar had poured beer down her front, he wasn't sure whether the jerk might do something stupid like follow her home.

"I went into the house, drank a bottle of wine, and passed out on the couch. I woke up yesterday with a hangover from hell."

"A whole bottle?"

"Yep." She scooped another shovelful, dumping it into the wheelbarrow before getting another one. "And then I talked to a potential trainer who came by on Sunday morning."

"Really? That's great."

"Yes. She is starting in two weeks from today."

His stomach knotted. *She?* "Uh, she?"

"Yep. Her name is Amy Montrose." She glanced his way as she stopped to lean on the shovel. "She's from here or close by. You might know her."

Hell yes, I know her and oh fucking hell no!

"Is there a problem?"

He cleared his throat, attempting to remove the lump that threatened to shut off his air. Amy. God, he didn't need to be around her. What if she did the same shit she had before? What if she caused problems? He didn't know what kind of a trainer she was, but he knew what she'd done before and he didn't want to have to deal with it. "I thought you were going to run any potential trainers by me?"

Her eyes narrowed as she focused on him. "Let's get something straight, Caleb. You work for me, not the other way around. I will hire the people I feel are best for the job, without consulting you, if I so choose."

He tipped his head back on his shoulders, staring at the rafters above his head for a moment. A sigh escaped his lips before he turned his gaze back on her. "You hired me to do a job. If you want to run this entire operation by yourself, that's fine with me. I can find another job." He turned on his heels, headed for his truck.

"Wait!"

He kept moving. He was done with this shit. Working for a woman would never work, not for him. Pride kept him from bowing at her feet. He was good, he knew that and he wasn't about to be a pansy for anyone, much less a woman who thought she knew how to run a ranch.

"Caleb, wait, please?"

His steps stopped as he made it to the front bumper. He didn't turn around as he waited for her to speak.

Silence stretched as he tapped his fingers on his thigh. He wasn't going to give on this, otherwise, he would never be able to run this place the way he knew it had to be run. Would she give him enough reins to do what needed to be done? He wasn't sure. He kind of liked her spunk and determination though.

Fingers touched the sleeve of his shirt.

"We need to come to some kind of compromise." She moved around so she was in front of him. "You have an expertise I don't have. I need you to help me, but we need to figure out how to work together."

It didn't take a genius to know he was attracted to her and it didn't help matters either. His gaze slid over her face noticing her high cheekbones, her long eyelashes, her crystal blue eyes, the pink lips that he was trying so desperately hard not to lean down and taste, and the long hair he wanted to wrap his hands in. She was stunning and he needed to get his head out from between his legs otherwise this would never work.

"Why is Amy such a problem for you?"

"She and I have a history."

"History?"

"We dated."

"It didn't end well, I assume?"

He debated to what to tell her. *The truth?* "It was a mutual parting, but there were some hard feelings."

"And?"

Shit. This wasn't going well. He wasn't sure he should tell her the entire thing. What if Amy found out he was to be her boss? What if she decided to bring up the problems they'd had before?

"Are you going to tell me, Caleb, or do I have to ask Amy?"

"Did you tell her I am the foreman here?"

"Yes, actually I did."

"And she didn't change her mind about the job?"

"No." Charlie jammed her hands on her hips and narrowed her eyes. "Tell me."

"All right. Fine." He took a few steps away as he pushed his hand through his hair and then settled his hat back on his head. "We dated. She got too attached and I bailed out of the relationship. I wasn't looking for permanent. She was. When I broke up with her, she trashed my truck."

"Trashed your truck?"

"She took a baseball bat to the headlights, slashed the tires, broke the windshield, and carved her name in my seats."

Charlie attempted to hide the grin threatening to spread across her face. She lost.

"It wasn't funny, Charlie. It cost several thousand dollars to fix."

"I'm sure."

"Now you know. I don't want any trouble from her and if we have to work together, that might be an issue."

"Are you?"

"Am I what?"

"Still working here?"

"That all depends on you and whether you are willing to work with me on hiring the help."

She stared off into the distance for a moment before her gaze came back to his face. "All right. We will interview and decide on the trainers together. I'm sure you know the people around here better than I do, so you can tell me if there are issues with them that I might not know about."

"True." He stuffed his hands into the front pockets of his jeans mostly to keep from reaching for her. Touching her would be a really bad idea all the way around and kissing her would be worse, but damn did he ever want to see how soft her lips were. "I'd better get to work."

"Yeah, I guess so." She rocked back on her heels for a second. "Caleb?"

"Yeah?"

"Thanks. I appreciate you staying to help me."

"You're welcome." He turned around and headed back for the barn debating on whether he'd done the right thing in the end. Staying here probably wasn't it, but he just couldn't seem to walk away from Charlie.

This is going to turn out badly, I'm afraid because wanting to touch her and kiss her is the worst possible thing I could do. Getting tied up with the boss is wrong on so many levels.

He stopped in the barn doorway and turned back toward the house. She'd taken the steps up to the front door but turned to look back at the barn.

When she lifted her hand in a wave, he couldn't help but return it.

Her smile was contagious as he grinned, wondering what the hell he'd just gotten himself into.

Chapter Four

Excitement made her whole body tingle as she bounced on her toes. She had been waiting all day for this delivery. The driver had called earlier telling her he'd be later in the day with his load. There had been an issue with the trailer and a flat tire.

The truck hauling her stallion turned around in the driveway so the trailer could be backed up toward the barn. She could see the majestic head of the animal through the opening on the side. He was magnificent.

The driver climbed out of the cab of his truck and walked toward her with a clipboard in his hands. "Charlie Abrams?"

"That's me."

The eyebrow over his left eye shot up to the rim of his hat. "You're Charlie Abrams?"

"Yes, I am."

He pushed the clipboard into her hands. "Sign here."

Her signature was nothing more than a scrawl across the page as she focused on the back of the trailer where Caleb was working the latches loose.

"Easy boy."

The tone of his voice and the slow, soft drawl had shivers skittering across her flesh. She rubbed her bare arms to calm the chills as she moved toward the back of the trailer. Caleb had hooked a lead rope onto the stallion's halter. His hands were sure as the stroked the animal's neck. *What would those hands feel like on my skin?* Did he have calluses on his fingers that would abrade as he moved them down her body? Her mouth went dry forcing her to lick her lips to moisten them so she could speak. "How does he look?"

Caleb's gaze darted to her for a moment before going back to the animal. "Perfect."

The horse's coat quivered as Caleb ran his hands over him again.

"Watch yourself. I'm going to back him out." He worked the horse loose from the tie downs and pulled his head down as he crooned softly, working the stallion to get him to step back out of the rear of the trailer.

The horse balked slightly as his hooves hit the metal ramp, causing him to step unsteadily. Caleb never moved from near his head, talking softly into the horse's ears and making sure the animal knew he was okay.

The moment the stallion stepped onto solid ground, his nervousness eased visibly as he dropped his head and pressed against Caleb's chest. "Good boy." It was obvious the animal and Caleb had bonded.

"He likes you."

Caleb lifted his gaze, catching hers across the small expanse of space between them. Even though his eyes were dark, she could see a few tiny flecks of green in them that caught the light. His lips lifted in a small smile as his hand continued to stroke the stallion's neck. "He is a gorgeous animal. He will do well for your stable."

"Thank you. I knew he would be perfect the moment I saw his picture. I had hoped he would be gentle. Stallion's aren't usually like that."

"Only when there are mares in heat around. Right now, there aren't any here, so he's calm. Don't get around him once the mares arrive."

"But he looks like a big baby."

His gaze narrowed. "He would kill you to get to a mare. Don't *ever* take his nature right now for granted."

Her heart sped up, slamming against her ribs as it raced along. Was he warning her? *Of course he is you ninny.* "I know. I've been around enough horses, Caleb."

He didn't move for a moment as he watched her, his gaze never leaving her face. Heat seared her body, making her tremble from only the look in his eyes. It said, don't try my patience or there will be consequences. He definitely wasn't a man to cross.

She licked her lips, causing him to lose his focus as his gaze went to her mouth.

"I'll stable him."

"Okay," she whispered, unsure of whether she should follow or leave him to put the stallion up himself. She chose the latter to give her a moment to catch her breath. Damn if he didn't cause her to lose her concentration whenever he was around. This wasn't good. He was an employee after all.

Her cell phone jingled in her back pocket, causing her butt to vibrate. When she pulled it out, she realized it was her father. "Hey, Dad."

"Hey, baby. Weren't you supposed to get your stallion today?"

"Yep. He just arrived a few moments ago. My foreman is stabling him now."

"How does he look?"

"Fantastic." She took a few steps toward the barn. "He's beautiful, Dad. I couldn't have asked for a better start to my breeding program."

"You'll have to send me some pictures."

"I will." She tucked a strand of hair behind her ear before shifting the phone to the other side and glancing into the dark interior of the barn. She could see Caleb moving around toward the stall they'd chosen to house the stallion until the mares arrived. The breadth of his shoulders almost stretched from one side of the opening to the other, making her realize he had a massive chest. *He needs that kind of strength to handle the horses.* He grabbed a large bale of hay, hefting it up on his shoulder. His shirt was pulled tight, emphasizing his pecs to perfect.

She hoped he didn't realize she was watching him. That would be so embarrassing.

"Charlie?"

"Oh, yeah, sorry. What did you say?"

"I asked if you were coming home for the holidays."

"Uh, probably not. Maybe Christmas, but not Thanksgiving. I need to be here to make sure things are taken care of."

"I thought you hired a foreman?"

"I did and he's great, but you know me. I'm a hands on type manager."

Her dad laughed a deep throaty chuckle that made her smile. "I know exactly what you mean, baby girl. You need to trust your guy though."

"I do, Dad. I trust him explicitly, but it's hard when we are just starting out."

"Have you hired any trainers yet?"

"Sort of. I have someone starting in a couple of weeks, but I need more."

"Go slow, honey. You only need one or two to start with until you get several horses ready to go."

"I know." Caleb came out of the stall, slide the door shut, and then engaged the bolt. "I should go, Dad. I need to talk to Caleb about something."

"Okay. I'll talk to you later, honey. Call me later this week."

"Will do. I love you."

"Love you too, baby girl."

"Bye." She hung up the phone and slid it into her pocket just as Caleb came through the double doors of the barn. "Is he settled?"

"As settled as he'd going to get for now. It'll take him a few days to get acclimated." He pushed his hat off his head before ramming his hand through the side of his hair. "When is Amy supposed to start?"

"We need to talk about that. Can you come up to the house?"

"Uh, I guess so. I have some other chores to do, but I can work on them this afternoon." He swept his hand to the side. "After you."

The driver pulling the trailer honked as he headed down her gravel driveway, waving his hand from the window as he disappeared out the gate.

She led the way toward the house with Caleb at her elbow. They stepped up on the porch at the same time. "Want to talk out here or inside?"

"Out here is fine."

The chairs in the corner would be good, neutral ground she guessed. She needed that with him around. Having him in her space probably wasn't a good idea with her thoughts going haywire all the time. "What are your thoughts on Amy's abilities to train?"

"I don't know. I can ask around, but I've never seen her work horses before."

"You obviously have an issue with her personally then."

"After what I told you before, I would think that's pretty apparent."

She tapped her fingers on the arm of the chair, concentrating on what he was saying rather than how much she liked his smile, especially when it was aimed at her. "I will talk with her and let her know about you being the foreman out here and see what she says. How long ago was this issue between you?"

"Two years ago."

"I would think she'd be over it by now. Are you?"

"Over her?"

Charlie shrugged, not sure if that's what she meant or not. "I guess so."

"I wasn't the one with the problem, Charlie. There was no getting over her since I wasn't invested in the relationship. It wasn't anything permanent. I was having fun, that's all."

"And she wanted more?"

"Yep." He adjusted his hat before focusing on her again. "I found out she was talking wedding dresses, rings, buying a house, and kids. I backed out of that faster than a thoroughbred taking off from the gate at the Kentucky Derby."

She couldn't help but smile at that metaphor. "I see."

Thunder rumbled in the distance. Several flashes of lightning lit up the darkening sky. "Looks like rain."

"Yeah. I wonder how the stallion will do."

"I guess we'll find out."

A couple of large raindrops hit the ground just outside the covering of the porch before it began to downpour in a sheet of rain. "Wow."

"We get these pretty often. It'll blow out in a little while." He climbed to his feet. "I'll go check on the stallion."

"You'll get soaked."

He turned his gaze on her when he reached the steps. "I won't melt, Charlie." With his hat tucked low on his head, he took off across the yard toward the barn.

Reaching the door safely, he turned to wave at her, giving her a gorgeous view of his chest with his shirt plastered to his flesh like a second skin. "Holy shit." His jeans were soaked as well, leaving very little to her imagination as he turned and went inside. Her breath came out quickly as she adjusted her spot on the chair. She blew out a heavy sigh when she climbed to her feet to go into the house. Dinner waited in the crock pot on the counter. A hearty beef stew sounded really good right now.

"Wine. Yeah, I need something to uncoil this feeling in my belly so I can sleep tonight."

Pretty depressing to think she'd be spending a Saturday night alone. *This is not a bad thing. I need to get myself together before I even think about having a man in my life.*

The door shut behind her as the rain battered the house, lashing against the sides in sheets. Thunder rumbled loudly, rattling the windows between streaks of lightning.

Storms were some of her favorite things. Listening to the rain pounding the roof, especially on this house since it had a tin roof. There was nothing like it.

After she scooped up some of the stew in a bowl, she grabbed a glass of wine, a couple of slices of bread, and took a seat at the long table that was made from reclaimed barn wood. She loved the table. It fit perfectly in the rough interior of the house. The floors were made of pine from what she could tell, but they'd been buffed to a high shine. The doorways had the same barn wood trim as the table, bringing the whole thing together. Cabinets lined the walls in the kitchen that were a deep green with an antiquing stain on them, and the counters were black granite with swirls of green in it.

A loud crack of thunder made her jump to her feet.

Nervous energy raced through her as she headed for the door. The stallion was probably going crazy in the stall.

She glanced at the hanger by the door, cursing herself for not unpacking her rain slicker. *Shit. I guess I'll have to go without it.*

When she opened the door, rain sliced sideways. Large puddles of water stood between her and the barn.

Knowing she was about to get soaked, she darted down the steps of the house and ran for the barn.

Her boots slipped in a large puddle, landing her on her backside in the water. *Damn it!* She ineffectively wiped at the rain streaming down her face. Her hair was now plastered to her scalp, her shirt was stuck to her skin, making it almost transparent, and her jeans were soaked through as well. Mud clung to her pants as she climbed to her feet. A shiver rolled through her when the wind decided to whip around her, throwing a large branch from a tree near the house, right across her path.

Picking up her pace, she ran for the barn.

The moment she hit the doorway, the water sluicing down her front, stopped. She blinked several times, trying to focus on the interior of the barn through the curtain of hair she had to push out of her face. A bare light bulb shined near the back where they'd stabled the stallion, so she made her way toward it.

Her teeth began to chatter as the temperature outside started to drop.

When she got near the stall, she looked inside hoping to find Caleb. He wasn't there, but the stallion stood happily munching on hay. "Well, I guess I didn't need to worry about you, now did I?"

The horse stuck his nose near the half-door, wanting a scratch or two.

Now she would have to wait until the rain slowed down a little before she could make her way back to the house. Of course, she was already soaked to the bone. What did it matter?

A soft twang of a guitar reached her ears, making her tilt her head to the side as she listened.

Following the sound, she moved toward the back of the barn where the ladder to the loft was. A deep baritone voice could be heard under the pounding rain.

She made her way up the ladder only to find Caleb sitting on a bale of hay strumming a guitar and humming along. Every few moments, he'd lean over and write something on the pad of paper near his knee.

He didn't see her as she moved a little closer listening to the sound of his voice.

Quietly, she took a seat on a hay bale several yards away. She didn't want to disturb him, but she liked the sound and wanted to listen.

Rain pounded on the roof of the barn, the accompanying tinging sound almost blended with the song Caleb was strumming, like a drum playing along with the tune.

When he played the entire song, singing the lyrics too, she was mesmerized. He had a beautiful voice. As the song came to an end, the last note drifting off into the silence now enveloping them, she held her breath waiting for something to happen.

The rain had stopped pounding down, only to hear an occasional plop on the roof. Unable to hold her breath any longer, she sighed.

His head whipped around as he spun on the hay bale.

"I'm sorry. I didn't mean to intrude."

He smiled as he dropped his gaze to the floor covered in hay. "I didn't know you were there."

"That was beautiful, Caleb. You have a magnificent voice. Do you sing professionally?"

"Nah. I write some stuff and sing my own, but not in front of people unless it's family or close friends."

"You should. You are really good."

"Thank you, but I just mess around. It's nothin'." His head came back up as his eyes narrowed. "You're soakin' wet."

A glance down at her shirt made her realize how see through the material was as she pulled it from her front. "Yeah. I got caught in the rain coming to the barn. I was worried about the stallion, but he's fine. The rain didn't seem to bother him at all."

"No. He's happy as a little pig in shit." He blushed a deep red. "Sorry. I shouldn't cuss in front of a lady."

She laughed out loud. "A lady, huh? Well, it's been a long time since I've been called that."

He set the guitar aside. "You'll get sick if you don't get some dry clothes on."

"It's okay. I was headed to the house when I heard you up here." She climbed to her feet. "Now that you are done, I'll go on inside take a warm bath, have a glass of wine, and snuggle down for the night." A cold breeze came through the open hay door behind Caleb and she shivered. Her nipples pulled into tight little nubs as the freezing material clung to her front.

Caleb's eyes darkened and his lips parted as he came to his feet. He quickly unbuttoned his shirt, moving toward her. "Here. Put this on to cover you until you get inside."

All of the saliva in her mouth dried up. Spit was nonexistent as she tried desperately to think of something to say that didn't sound really stupid. Her gaze went to his chest and the smattering of hair that made a little trail to the waistband of his jeans. *Oh, God.* He had a real honest to goodness six pack. His jeans hung low on his hips, emphasizing the trim, leanness of his waist. "I can't take your shirt. You'll freeze."

"I have another one down in the tack room. I'll be okay, but you need to get warmed up." He brought it around her shoulders.

The scent of him clung to the material, something musky and warm. She closed her eyes at his nearness, wanting nothing more than to reach out her hand and touch his skin. Trying frantically to keep her head, she opened her eyes and glanced up. *Oh shit.* He looked down at the same time.

His hands were on her upper arms, the heat scalding her through the material. His lips were so close, too close. If she moved slightly, she could almost reach them with hers. The air sizzled around them as if the whole place was charged from the electrical storm that had rolled through earlier.

"Caleb, I—"

"Should go."

"Yes, yes. I should go." She stepped back out of his embrace, almost stumbling as she headed for the ladder and the safety of the bottom floor of the barn.

The stallion knickered as she reached the ground and almost ran for the house, her steps quick and sure while she avoided the biggest of the puddles.

The rain had stopped and the night sky had cleared. Stars blinked above her head and the air was much cooler than it had been earlier in the day.

A creak of the steps on the porch announced her arrival at the door. *Inside. Inside.*

The door had been left open when she'd run for the barn. Luckily the rain had not soaked the floor.

Unable to stop herself, she turned and looked back. Caleb stood at the arched doorway with his hand on the doorjamb, watching her silently. He didn't raise his hand, he only watched as she moved inside and shut the door.

Cold seeped through the shirt when she pressed her back to the door. Panting hard, she pressed her fingers to her lips wanting nothing more than the pressure of his mouth against hers. *Damn it! I can't do this. I won't do this. The last thing I need is to get tangled up with my foreman.*

Her boots were cold and wet on her feet and she was leaving a puddle on the floor near the front door. *I need to get dry before I get sick.* She toed off her boots, leaving them where they landed by the door. Stripping his shirt off her shoulders, she held it by the collar for a moment debating on what to do with it. The least she could do would be to wash it since he offered it for warmth.

She stood there for a few seconds before she slowly brought the shirt to her nose. His scent clung to the material and she felt herself sink into his smell. The musk, sweat, and something tangy had her imagining touching his bare chest she'd seen when he taken off his shirt. Being able to run her hands down and across those ridges on his abdomen had her thoughts going haywire.

"This is not good, not good at all. I need to get myself under control before I do something really stupid like invite him into my bed." She pushed off the wall headed for the laundry room. The wet clothes reminded her that she needed to get out of them and warm up.

She pushed the door open and flipped on the light. Her washer and dryer sat against the wall with the huge racks above them to hold her detergent, bleach, and whatnots she needed to wash her clothes.

Her jeans hit the floor in a plop as she stripped them off along with her shirt. A shiver rolled through her, making her realize it was chilly in the house. She probably needed to turn on the heat. Evenings could still be cool in Texas in October.

After she put her clothes in along with Caleb's shirt, she poured in some soap and hit the start button. She probably should have put in more dirty clothes, but she didn't feel like going into her room to get them right at the moment.

The bathroom off the laundry room afforded her the luxury of getting a hot shower before putting on her fluffy bathrobe. She could put underwear on when she went to bed. It felt rather naughty not wearing underwear. It didn't matter though. Not that anyone would know except her.

She turned on the spigot inside the enclosed shower, laid out the bathrobe, and then climbed inside as she let the water slide over her. With her head tipped back, the liquid sluiced down her back in long rivulets, soothing away the day's labors.

Once she grabbed the soap to wash the grime away, she let her hands linger over her breasts. Self-gratification had become a norm for her since her divorce, but even then, it felt a little wicked to bring herself to orgasm. Right now, she needed it though, badly. She'd been drenched from being near Caleb and almost kissing him that she was wound up tighter than a strand of barbed wire strung around a fence post.

This will have to do since getting involved with him is a really bad idea.

She skimmed her hands over her breasts as she closed her eyes. The image of Caleb standing in front of her rose behind her eyelids and when she slipped her fingers around her nipples, she could imagine him running his tongue around one while he palmed the other. A soft moan escaped her lips.

One hand slid down her abdomen, delving between her pussy lips to glance off her clit. Her hips jerked forward as she continued to flick her clit with her finger. The little button was sensitive and it took very little effort on her part to bring herself to the brink of climax.

Her body went rigid, but she couldn't quite make herself go over the edge.

Something held her back.

"Damn it!"

She continued to try to bring herself to climax for several minutes, but as the water began to cool, she gave up, shut the water off, and opened the door to the shower. Steam rolled out, fogging the mirror. The rug under her feet was soft against her soles when she stepped out.

Wine would be her friend tonight and maybe some porn. That always seemed to work in her favor.

Her life really sucked at the moment if she was going to have to masturbate to watching someone else have sex.

"Great." She shook her head, pulled on her bathrobe and headed for the kitchen to find the wine.

Saturday nights like this were made for alcohol and book boyfriends.

Chapter Five

The next morning when she opened her eyes, her world spun. Dizziness engulfed her and before she could blink, she jumped out of her bed and ran to the bathroom.

Retching was one her of her least favorite things to do, but here she was throwing up her guts into the toilet. Was it the wine? No. She hadn't drank that much, only a glass or two before she'd warmed up, got sleepy, and went on to bed.

The coolness of the toilet bowl felt like heaven against her cheek. Was that weird? Maybe, but she didn't care. Right now, she felt like hell. Her head pounded like someone was picking away at her brain from the inside, her throat hurt even when she swallowed, and her body ached from the roots of her hair to the soles of her feet.

"Oh my God." She moaned as she closed her eyes and willed the spinning room to stop.

If she could just make it back to her bed, she could go back to sleep and wake up feeling better. Her whole body shook from head to toe as goose bumps skittered across her flesh. She was freezing.

"Something. I need Tylenol or a new head. God, I hurt."

She forced herself to her feet and staggered to the medicine chest. Two Tylenol would be the ticket for now and rest, lots of rest.

When she'd taken the pills, she crawled beneath the blanket, turned up the heat on her bed, and fell into a deep sleep.

Sunlight forced her to open her eyes as her head pounded. Gritty and caked with gunk, she cracked them before slamming them shut again.

The pounding continued until she realized it was someone at the front door.

She coughed until her chest felt like it would split open before forcing herself to her feet.

The door. I need to answer the door.

Her stumbling steps took her down the hallway until she'd almost reached the door. She had to stop and brace herself against the doorjamb as her head swam.

"Charlie?"

Oh God. "Caleb?" Her voice came out in a strangled whisper.

He opened the door. "Charlie, where are you?"

"Here." She slid to the floor.

He moved like lightning and before she could blink, he was kneeling next to her. "Honey, you look like shit."

"Thanks."

His hand on her forehead was cool to the touch. "You are running one hell of a fever, darlin'. Let me get you to bed."

He scooped her up in his arms, cradling her against his chest as he moved down the hallway toward her bedroom. How he knew which one was hers, she didn't know, nor did she care at the moment.

The bed was soft and warm as he laid her down and covered her up with the blankets until she could barely see over them.

His steps echoed on the wood floor when he headed for the bathroom. He was back in seconds, holding her behind the shoulders so she could take more medicine. "Tylenol. How long have you been like this?"

"I don't know." Her voice came out in a scratching croaking noise. "Since it rained?"

"Darlin', that was two days ago."

"Two days?"

"Yeah. I didn't think anything about not seein' you yesterday, but when you didn't make an appearance again today, I got worried." He pressed his hand to her cheek. "Have you eaten or drank anything?"

"No. I've done nothing but sleep apparently."

He stood next to the bed. "Do you have any soup, juice, or anything like that in the kitchen?"

"No."

His keys jingled as he took them out of his pocket. "I'll be right back. I'm going to run into town and get some supplies. Don't move. Go back to sleep or something until I get back. You need to rest."

He moved toward the door but stopped when she said his name. "Caleb?"

"Yeah?"

"Thank you."

He tipped his hat and shut the door behind him.

When she drifted off to sleep, she dreamed of him lying beside her, his hands wandering over her body and bringing her to the peak of desire before he crawled between her legs. His big hands held down her hips when his tongue dipped between her pussy lips finding her clit hard and swollen with desire. She moaned as she rolled to her back, throwing her arm up over her head. The calluses on his palms abraded her skin deliciously, something she'd never felt before. Her nipples hardened into tight little points, wanting his mouth there too. "Caleb, please, I need you," she whispered pulling at his shoulders to bring him up so he would slide his thick cock inside her. His lips raked along her neck, his whiskered jaw scraping against her skin as she shivered from the sensation. When his length pushed into her, she sighed loving the feeling of him there. "Oh yes. That's it. Fuck me."

* * * *

Caleb stood at the doorway of her bedroom with a bowl of soup in one hand and a glass of ginger ale in the other. She could tell she was sleeping by the steady rise and fall of her chest, but she needed to eat and drink something. If she'd been out for two days, she was probably dehydrated as well.

"Oh yes. That's it. Fuck me."

Her words stopped him in his tracks. "What the hell?" he whispered.

She twisted her legs back and forth under the covers, lifting her hips as if someone was in the bed with her under the covers. A moan reached his ears and what he thought was his name.

Not sure what to do, he moved to her bedside and set the bowl and glass down before he dropped them. He removed his hat and set it down on the chair. Waking her up would be the best thing, he figured, but how to do it without startling her or whatever.

What a gaggle-fuck.

He dragged his hand through his hair as he moved a little closer and said her name softly.

She didn't awaken but groaned deep in her throat like she was in the throes of a passionate embrace.

Damn. This is crazy.

He touched her shoulder and shook her lightly while he said her name again.

"Caleb, kiss me. I need you."

Kissing her was a really bad idea. He'd wanted to do that since the moment he'd seen her, but she was sick, really sick, and this was totally stupid. When they'd been face to face in the barn a few days ago, her lips had looked so soft and inviting, all he wanted to do was press his mouth to hers. Totally the wrong thing to do. She was his boss after all and it would get really weird if they were to have any kind of a fling, but damn it he wanted her like his next breath.

Needing a moment away from her temptation, he went into the bathroom and grabbed a washcloth so he could wet it and put it on her forehead. She needed to cool down in more ways than one. He figured this whole thing going on right now was delirium from the fever. That sounded plausible and she probably didn't even realize what she was saying and doing.

"Right. Okay. Cool washcloth." He wrung it out until it had stopped dripping and took it into the bedroom.

When he reached her side, her eyes were open and bright with fever. "Caleb?"

"Yeah. I brought you some soup and ginger ale. You need something in your stomach."

"I feel like shit."

"I'm sure, but this will make you feel better." He pressed the washcloth to her head and she moaned softly.

"Thank you. That feels wonderful."

"Can you sit up to eat?"

"I don't know. My head wants to swim when I sit up."

After he toed off his boots, he got behind her, lifting her shoulders until he could sit and let her relax against his chest. "I'll brace your back so you can eat." The cup with the soup in it was brought in front of her as he helped her bring it to her mouth. "Sip it. It's just broth, but you need the liquid."

The heat from her body almost scalded him, she was so hot, but he knew the Tylenol would help in a few moments as soon as it kicked in.

"Caleb?"

"Yeah?"

"I'm sorry to be such a bother."

"You aren't. I'm sorry you are sick. I should have checked on you yesterday." She coughed so hard, she shook the bed. Her breath came out in a rattle and he knew that wasn't good even without medical training. "You should probably go to the hospital. You sound terrible."

"I'll be fine. I just need to rest. I'm so tired." Her voice was low and soft sounding, almost a whisper.

He took the cup from her hand, putting it on the nightstand.

A soft snore met his ear a few moments later and he realized she'd fallen asleep on his chest.

He touched her cheek with his fingertips to find it a bit cooler. Hopefully her fever would come down now, but how in the hell was he going to get out from beneath her to let her sleep in peace?

His head banged against the wall with an easy thump, thump while he tried to think of how to get out of this mess. He had work to do in the barn, except moving right now seemed impossible. Charlie's curves pressed against him in the most delicious way, something he wasn't prepared to handle at the moment. His cock hardened behind the fly of his jeans. *Not a good idea right now.*

He let his mind wander a little, thinking about things he needed to get accomplished this week.

Clean out the stallion's stall.

Make sure the water troughs were all in good shape.

Check the fences.

Shore up the stalls in the barn.

Her lips would be soft under his, he just knew it. She would moan as he touched her, skimming his hands from her shoulders to her hips. Her hair would slip through his fingers like water cascading off rocks. *Oh shit. This isn't good.*

She shifted against him, rubbing her cute little butt against his groin. *Holy hell! I need to get out from behind her.*

A shiver rolled through her, making him realize her fever probably broke, but now she'd be freezing.

Crap.

He reached down and pulled the blanket up around her shoulders, cocooning them in like two peas in a pod. The heat would probably kill him as it wrapped around them.

The sun began to set behind the shades on her window as his stomach grumbled. He hadn't eaten since this morning, early, now his empty insides were making it known. It would have to wait. He needed to take care of Charlie at the moment, even though he wasn't sure why. It wasn't like he was family or anything. She didn't have anyone here though, that he knew of. No friends and no family.

"So cold," she whispered, turning in his arms so she was snuggled against his chest with her cheek resting on his pecs.

"Oh God," he murmured, willing his body to not react to her nearness.

Her warm breath managed to get inside the opening of his shirt, wafting across his skin and bringing up goose bumps on his flesh. She was practically lying on top of him and it wasn't good. In the next breath, he realized it was *really* good because her hip was cradled against his groin and her right breast was pressed against his chest.

Knowing he wasn't going anywhere anytime soon, he lifted his hat off his head, tossing it on the floor. He might as well get comfortable.

He worked himself down in the bed, taking her with him until he was lying flat on the mattress with her lying on top of him. Her breathing was slow and even. Her skin felt warm, but not too hot. Luckily, she slept now.

His gaze found a crack in the ceiling above his head, tracing it toward the wall to the right. How in the hell he'd gotten himself in this mess, he wasn't sure. The last place he needed to be was underneath Charlie unless they were both naked. That couldn't happen if he was to keep this a business relationship.

Good Lord did he want her something fierce. He'd been fascinated from the moment he'd seen her in the pasture. Since then, it had only gotten worse. He'd fantasized about her while showering, dreaming about her while he slept, and seeing her face when he'd kissed other women.

He let his hand skim down her back as he glanced down at her sleeping form. She wore a thin nightgown that left little to the imagination. Her hair was matted and stuck to her head from the fever. Her skin was soft beneath his hand, making him think of silk.

She sighed and rubbed her face against his chest as he moved his hand to her hip.

Her lips grazed his skin where his shirt had opened slightly.

Holy fuck!

* * * *

Charlie opened her eyes to find a dark room. It had to be past midnight, but she wasn't sure where she was. There was very little light in the room except for a slight sliver coming through the shades on the window.

The surface under her rose and fell.

Her thoughts were jumbled. She couldn't remember anything after Caleb came in the front door, swept her up in his arms, and carried her to her room.

Caleb. Oh shit!

She moved her head slightly so she could look up. The scruff along his jaw scratched her forehead as she moved. He looked like he was asleep, his long eyelashes rested against his cheeks and his breathing was even and slow. His shirt beneath her body was soft like flannel and she could feel the hard muscles of his chest resting against her side. His belt buckle cut into her hip where she laid against his abdomen, but she didn't want to move. His arms were wrapped around her as if she was precious and he needed to protect her. The thought was nice even though it was very farfetched. He didn't even like her.

"How do you feel?" he asked softly as he shifted slightly under her.

"Like I've been hit by a truck."

"You were pretty sick."

"I don't remember much."

"I can imagine."

She laid her head back down on his chest, unwilling to relinquish being in his arms. "Thank you for taking care of me. I don't know what I would have done had you not come to find me."

"My pleasure."

After a moment or two, she said, "How did you end up under me? Not that I mind the position, but it is rather awkward since I'm your boss."

A soft chuckle left his lips. "I helped you sit up to drink some soup by sitting behind you. You fell asleep against me."

"I'm sorry."

"I'm not."

She wasn't sure what that meant. The two of them together outside of their working relationship would be a bad thing, right? Confusion seemed to be the sentiment today and how the hell to extricate herself from the position she was in should be her priority.

Not at the moment it wasn't.

His fingers moved over her back and she realized she had very little on. She loved the feeling of his hands on her skin and if she wasn't careful, she'd lose herself in the feel of him beneath her.

She ran her tongue over her teeth. *Yuck!* "Uh, I need a shower, I think." She put her hands on his chest and pushed herself into an upright position. Her head felt a little dizzy, but she figured she could make it on her own. Once she sat on the side of the bed, she moved to stand, swaying slightly on her feet.

"Do you need me to help you?"

"No, I think I can get it. It might take a minute to get in there, but washing my hair and stuff should be doable." She glanced at the window before she looked down at the bedside table, reading the clock. Eleven thirty. "It's the middle of the night? How long have I been laying on you?"

"About six hours, I guess, give or take."

"I am so sorry, Caleb. You should have just moved me and gone on home. I would have been okay."

"No way was I leaving you here in the shape you were in." He climbed to his feet beside her, touching her cheek with his fingertips. "You look much better. The fever seems to be gone and your head is clearer."

"Thanks to you."

"I did what anyone would do."

"I doubt that, but thank you anyway." She let her gaze roam over his face. His cheeks and jaw were covered by scruff that looked soft and prickly at the same time. Her fingertips itched to touch it. His lips were full, with the bottom one being a little bit larger than the top. His nose was straight with a slight flare to the nostrils. When she stopped at his eyes, she was lost in the look there. His irises had darkened to a deep blue, almost the color of the sea. She saw desire and need warring in his eyes, as if he wanted to touch her, but he was afraid to cross that line. "I should go shower," she whispered, almost forgetting what needed to be done.

"If you think you'll be okay, I'm going to go on home. Sunrise comes early."

"You can come over later if you want. You've been here all night."

"I'll be here early. There's work that needs to be done before the mares arrive."

"Thank you again for taking care of me."

"You're welcome." He bent down and retrieved his hat from the floor. "Sleep well and I'll see you in the morning."

"Night, Caleb."

"Night, Charlie."

She watched him grab his boots from the floor and head toward the door. He stopped for a moment, looking back over his shoulder as she wrapped her arms around herself, missing the feel of him against her. A chill ran through her. He'd been so warm touching her skin and holding her while she'd slept. The loss was almost painful.

When the door shut behind him, she released the sigh she'd been holding inside. It would be all kinds of wrong to get tangled up with him. He was her employee after all, but the thought of keeping things just friends between them seemed like a big mistake.

"No. I don't need a man in my life. I can take care of myself fine and when and if I get this ranch up and running the way it should be, I'll worry about my love life. Until then, work around here needs to be done." She nodded her head as if to convince herself before she grabbed some clean clothes and moved toward the bathroom. A nice warm shower would feel fabulous and hopefully relax her enough so she could sleep tonight. She had to hope her dreams wouldn't be invaded by thoughts of Caleb though. There had been some pretty vivid ones while she'd been delirious with fever. Good grief it would be really embarrassing if he knew where her thoughts had gone while she'd been dreaming of him.

She'd never lived it down if he'd known.

Chapter Six

Their tenuous relationship continued for the next week. They'd pass in the barn, exchange pleasantries, and continue on their way. Never mind the times she'd watch him from the kitchen window as he did his work cleaning stalls, repairing things, and feeding the animals already there.

After her bout with the flu, she'd gone into town and bought some chickens from the feed store, and two pygmy goats from a neighbor. She did spend some of her time out with the goats babying them and feeding them, but she didn't know that much about taking care of goats or chickens for that matter. She was a horse girl after all.

Amy would be arriving in a few moments to talk with her about working with Caleb. She wasn't looking forward to that conversation. It seemed all kinds of wrong to dig into their past relationship. It must be done though. She needed to get some trainers in here and they needed to be able to take orders from Caleb.

Later this week she planned to go horse shopping. She had several staked out that she thought would be a good addition to her stable that were green, unbroken, or in need of more training than their current owners wanted to give. It is kind of like flipping houses. Put the work in and sell for a profit. *I wonder if I should take Caleb. One or two of these might be overnight trips and that could get awkward.*

A knock on the door told her Amy had arrived. She took a deep breath in, letting it out in a slow exhale to calm her nerves.

When she opened the door, she found the pretty blonde standing on her doorstep.

"Hi, Amy."

"Hello."

Charlie pushed open the screen. "Come on in. I'd like to talk to you about the position I hired you for."

"There isn't a problem is there? I'm looking forward to starting."

"No. Not really, but there is something we need to talk about that might be a problem for you."

Amy took several steps into the house before turning toward her.

"Follow me. We can talk in my office."

Charlie led the way down the hall toward the small bedroom she commandeered for her ranch office. She went around the desk, indicating to Amy to take a chair across from her. When she sat down, she noticed Amy looking around before her gaze came back to her. "Can you tell me a little about your experience as a trainer for cutting horses?"

"I've worked around horses my entire life. My parents own a ranch, but they've retired from training. I have been working with cutting horses since I could walk and there have been several I've trained that have gone on to win some great awards."

"So why aren't you working at an established ranch?"

"It's hard for a woman to break into the business. If you noticed, most of the trainers are men."

"Yes, I realized that some time ago. Most of the ranches are owned by men as well and the riders are men. Seems a bit lopsided to me."

Amy smiled. "Me too. It is what it is. I hope you will still hire me."

Charlie tented her fingers, bringing the tips to under her chin. "There may be something that might change your mind about working here."

"I can't imagine what."

"My foreman is Caleb Armstrong. I understand you two have a history."

Amy's gaze shot to the window before coming back to her. "You mentioned that when we talked before."

"I wanted to give you the opportunity to back out of our arrangement before things got awkward if there is a problem. Caleb was hired before I even got here myself and from what I understand, he's the best."

"He is."

Silence stretched between them for several moments. The ticking of the clock on the wall was the only thing Charlie heard as she watched emotions ripple across Amy's face. Not sure what it meant, she gave the other woman time to come to terms with her feelings. The decision to let Amy talk didn't come easy. Charlie really didn't want to know what happened between the two of them.

"I guess I should explain."

"That's probably a good idea if you want to stay on here."

"Caleb and I dated a couple of years ago. I fell in love with him. He didn't reciprocate those feelings."

"Are you still in love with him?"

Amy climbed to her feet and moved toward the window. "You know. Until right now, I wasn't sure. If someone would have asked me that even a few days ago, I would probably have said maybe, but being forced to look inside myself and examine my heart knowing he's outside somewhere has given me the strength to say no, I'm not. I don't think I ever really was. I liked him a lot, don't get me wrong. He was everything I wanted in a husband." She turned back to face where Charlie sat. A smile lifted the corners of her mouth. "I am with a great guy now. We've dated for some time and I can't imagine my life without him in it. The way I feel when he's with me is so different from what I felt with Caleb, it's like night and day. I think now I can say Caleb is just a friend."

Charlie released a breath she hadn't been aware she'd been holding. "Good. I'm glad to hear you say that because I want you to work here, but I didn't want anything to be difficult since you'll be reporting to Caleb."

"It's okay. I think Caleb and I will be okay."

"Do you know of any other trainers looking for work? I need to hire a couple more to start with."

"Actually, I might. I do have a couple of people that might be looking. I'll get in touch with them and give them your number."

"That would be great." Charlie climbed to her feet and came around the desk. "Your shift starts Monday morning at eight. I have a horse being delivered this weekend that I would like you to start working with immediately. He's from my dad's place and one I had been working with for a bit, but I ran out of time. My dad is shipping him to me so we can work with him here. He's fast, agile, and a great prospect. I do have a couple more horses coming in that won't be mine. We will be training them for competition though."

Amy held out her hand. "Thank you for believing in me, Charlie. I won't let you down. I promise and I won't make things difficult with Caleb."

"I appreciate that and I'm glad to have you here."

After Amy had walked out of the office and she heard the front door close, Charlie took her seat behind the desk again before leaning back and closing her eyes. *The whole conversation could have been really awkward.* She was happy that things would be okay with Amy and Caleb and hopefully, Amy would send some more trainers their way.

A knock on the window next to her heard made her scream before she spun around to see Caleb's face through the screen. "You scared the shit out of me."

He smiled a panty-melting grin that lifted the corners of his mouth and revealed a hidden dimple in his left cheek. "Sorry."

"Come on in. The back door is open."

"Be right there."

Moments later, he stood in the doorway of her office looking like the cowboy he was from his button down blue shirt, to his jeans that hugged his lean hips, to his dusty cowboy boots on his feet and his straw cowboy hat on his head. *Damn, he looks good.*

She cleared her throat as he moved inside the room and the air seemed to be sucked right out. Breathing became a luxury, one she wasn't sure she had at the moment.

"Are you feeling all right? Your face looks flush."

"Uh, no. I'm fine. It's just warm in here." She grabbed a pad of paper from her desk and moved it back and forth in front of her face, attempting to cool her heated flesh. "Please, have a seat."

"Thanks." He crossed his right leg over his left knee at the ankle and leaned back in the leather chair. "I saw Amy leave."

"Yeah."

"So?"

"We talked and she's fine with working under your guidance. She told me what happened from her point of view and she's over it. She's with a guy she really likes now, and I think she'll be able to handle having you for her boss." Charlie took a drink from the glass of water she had sitting on the edge of her desk. Her throat was parched and dry as the desert or was it the way Caleb looked at her, she wasn't sure which. The heat in his eyes seemed to scorch her skin, branding her as if he touched her.

He didn't talk, didn't say a word, just watched her with those hooded eyes, not giving her an inch, not telling her anything about what was going on behind his gaze.

Her heart raced, thudding wildly in her chest. She licked her lips, trying desperately to keep herself on an even keel.

He got to his feet, slowly pushing off the arm of the chair, before moving around the edge of her desk.

She turned the chair so she could keep him in her line of sight.

He leaned toward her, his hands on the arms of her chair, making her tip back to continue to look into his eyes.

Was he going to kiss her? God, she hoped so, but then again, she didn't. That would confuse things and make it difficult to keep their employer/employee relationship. She wanted to feel his mouth on hers, to taste his kiss, to see if he kissed as good as she'd imagined.

His breath flittered across her lips, making them tingle while she waited for the pressure.

He reached behind her, taking a book off the shelf before standing tall and returning to his chair.

Her feet hit the floor with a thump. Disappoint curled tight in her chest, making it hard to breathe. *I need to get over this. I can't have a relationship with him. I don't want a relationship of any kind, much less from someone who is all about the short term.* She turned her chair and glanced out the window, taking in the paddock and the barn. All hers and it meant the world to her that she'd done this on her own, without her family. It was a beginning, one she needed to do to stand on her own two feet. A man was the last thing she needed clogging up her mind and making her think of things like love, family, kids, and forever.

* * * *

Caleb had seen how her lips parted as he got close. She wanted him to kiss her and by God, he wanted that too, but he hadn't. Why, he wasn't sure. Maybe it was the look in her eyes, the uncertainty, the skittishness, or fear he'd seen. She was afraid for some reason and that bothered him. Was she afraid of him? He would never hurt her, not if he had any choice in the matter.

He hadn't known her long, but it was long enough to know that he liked her a whole hell of a lot, and that meant something to him.

Until now, he'd never even thought about women other than an occasional roll in the hay and someone to appease the ache in his groin. With Charlie, it was different. She was strong and determined, something he hadn't realize drew him to her.

She looked out the window now as he sat across from her, staring at something outside only she could see, leaving him to wonder what was going through her mind.

He had seen her heartbeat fluttering wildly in her throat when he'd neared. She reacted that way before as he'd gotten close, so she must feel the attraction between them the same way he did. Air sizzled when they were near each other, making him realize how much he wanted to touch her.

Having her lean into him the other day when she'd been sick, seemed like forever ago. At the same time, he wanted that closeness again more than anything.

He turned the book over in his palm that he'd retrieved from the bookshelf behind her. *Training Cutting Horses.*

He smiled. He'd wanted to see what information he might be able to glean from the pages. Training horses had been his life from as long as he could remember, but when you look at it from someone else's point of view, there was always something new to learn. "Charlie?"

"Yes?" she replied, not turning to face him. Instead, she kept her eyes focused outside.

"I appreciate you talking to her. I hope things will be all right while she works here."

Charlie finally turned to face him. Her cheeks were flush with color and her gaze fixed on the desk in front of her like she didn't want to meet his eyes. She ran her tongue across the surface of her lips and his heart rate spiked. He loved when she did that. It made him focus on her mouth as he tried desperately to think of what else to say.

Finally, her gaze strayed to his face. Her eyes gave her away though. The uneasiness she was feeling was very evident in her eyes. "I have a horse arriving at the end of the week I want her to start with. He's one that I worked with on my dad's place, but I ran out of time. He's a good prospect and will be a good first horse for us to market."

"Sounds good." He climbed to his feet. "You don't mind if I borrow this, do you? I would like to read it and see if there are any new ideas I might be able to try when the new horses arrive."

She glanced at the book, tilting her head sideways to read the title. "No, of course. Go right ahead. It's one of my favorites."

A chuckle left his mouth. "You don't read fiction or anything for pleasure?" He turned the book over in his hand a couple of times. "This is pretty heavy reading."

"Not for a girl raised around cutting horses."

He tipped his head, acknowledging her statement. "I suppose not then." He turned and headed for the door. He needed some room to breathe. The air between them seemed to close in on him, pushing him to want to touch her, kiss her, run his fingers through her hair, and then lay her out on her desk and find out if she was as receptive to his touch as he wanted her to be. Lord, he had it bad. "I'll see you at supper."

"Caleb?"

"Yeah?"

A split second of silence turned him back toward her, giving him a sweet view of her breasts. *Crap. I need to get my head out of the gutter and leave her alone.*

"I'll be going into town to the feed store for supplies. Do you want to go with me?" She stood and leaned on her hands that were flat on the desktop. "I mean you could probably help me decide which brands are best for the breeds we will be working with. There are so many."

"Sure." Why in the hell he'd agreed to go with her, he didn't know. The more time he spent around her, the more he wanted her beneath him with her hands clutching at his back, her fingernails digging into his skin, and her legs wrapped around his waist. "What time?"

"After supper is fine. No rush. I have some accounting stuff to go over so I know how much money I have to spend. I have to pinch pennies where I can until we make our first sale."

"Got it. See you after while then."

"Yep."

He pulled the door shut behind him before he headed toward the front of the house. The coolness of the barn would be a welcome relief from the constant heat simmering between them when they were in the same room. His fingertips itched to touch her and feel her flesh under his hands. He wanted to see her eyes drift shut as he slid inside her hot center. Her mouth would be so sweet under his, he could almost taste her on his tongue.

Damn, he had it bad.

His steps took him across the lawn to the barn, down the walkway, and into the tack room. His balls ached like he hadn't had sex in years. To tell the truth, it made been a while, but still, he shouldn't be this horny except that when he was around Charlie, he couldn't even think of another woman much less bring a face to mind. He needed relief and badly, otherwise, he would do something really stupid like kiss her.

The door shut behind him when he pushed it closed with his foot. If he planned on spending a couple of hours with her this afternoon going into town, he needed to take the edge off the burning low in his gut.

The rolling desk chair sat tucked under the edge of the desk. It would have to do if he was going to find relief from this ache.

The soothing, earthy scent of leather permeated the air, the familiar fragrance a welcome touch, mixed with the odor of horses, hay, and dirt. His place in the world revolved around these aromas. Nothing in his life brought more comfort than these. He was a cowboy after all.

He moved toward the desk, grabbing his belt buckle in his hand to unlatch it from where it rested at his waist. The clink of metal sounded loud in the small room. His jeans pooled at the ankles after he unbuttoned them and pushed them down, letting them gather around his boots.

His naked ass hit the cold plastic of the chair. This seemed totally wrong, but he needed to get her out of his system at least temporarily.

He palmed his dick, wrapping his fist completely around his rock hard cock. A moan escaped his lips as he closed his eyes, leaned back in the chair, and imagined Charlie on her knees between his thighs.

Her eyes were fixed on his face as she took the head of his cock in her mouth. The warmth surrounding him felt amazing. Her lips were shiny and wet when she licked him from base to tip while her hand engulfed his girth, meeting her mouth on the way down. Her head bobbed up and down as she continued to suck him.

She moaned softly, taking him to the back of her throat. The vibration almost sent him over the edge into the oblivion of climax.

"I want you inside me, Caleb. I want to feel you so deep, it almost hurts, but hurts so good I can't help from coming all over you."

"Fuck yeah."

His hand moved faster over his length, squeezing and rubbing hard enough he couldn't hold back his orgasm any more than he could wait to fuck Charlie. Cum shot out the end of his dick, squirting thick, white cream all over his abdomen.

His breath came out in raspy, panting breaths as his heart slammed against his rib cage. It has been a long time since he'd had an orgasm that intense, especially self-produced. Blood thrummed in his ears, blocking out all sound except the whooshing.

A knock sounded on the tack room door. "Caleb?"

Oh hell! He jumped up, stuffing his soft dick back into his jeans. "Just a second." *Did I lock the door? God, I hope I did.* He glanced at the lock, realizing yes, he did turn it so the knob was secure. *Thank God.*

"Are you okay?"

"Yeah. I was cleaning some tack and I have oil on my hands. I need to clean it off before I can open the door. Hang on." He quickly wiped the cum from his hands and shirt on an oily towel on the table. The black substance left a film on his palms. "Shit."

Charlie knocked on the door. "Caleb?"

"Just a second, Charlie. I need to find something to wipe this off with that doesn't already have oil on it."

He grabbed a dirty paper towel from the trashcan, rubbing his hands on it to try to get as much off as he could. The scent of oil was strong in the room now, and he hoped it would block out the smell of cum.

When he glanced around the room, he figured it was clean enough to keep her from realizing what he was doing in there before he opened the door. She stood on the other side with a white peasant blouse, jeans tucked into the tops of her cowboy boots, and a smile on her face.

"I figured we could grab something to eat in town instead of eating here, since it's only you and me, before we go to the feed store."

"Uh, yeah. Sounds good. Let me grab my keys."

She tilted her head to the side as she glanced down his front. "Why is your shirt untucked and your belt loose?"

"I, uh—" *Shit. What the hell am I supposed to say? I can't say I was jacking off to images of you sucking me off. No, that wouldn't be a good idea.* "I spilled some of the oil on my jeans. I didn't want to go to town with oil all over them, so I changed."

"You have a pair of clean jeans in the tack room?"

"Uh, yeah. I always keep a clean pair with me in case I get really dirty cleaning stalls or whatever, especially if I'm headed out right after work. I don't want to have to run home to change."

"If you hand me your dirty ones, I'll wash them. I have a load to go in right now anyway."

Well, fuck me sideways. Now what the hell do I say?

Chapter Seven

"Come on, Caleb. Give me your dirty jeans and I'll wash them for you."

He sighed, dropping his gaze to the dirt floor at his feet as he put his hands on his hips. "I can't."

"What? Why not?"

Tell her? Don't tell her? "Okay, it's like this, Charlie. I wasn't oiling tack."

"What were you doing then?"

"You'll think it's weird or something."

She stepped closer and placed her hand on his arm. "No, I won't. Tell me."

He brought his hands up to cup her face, running his thumbs over her cheekbones. "I've been imagining kissing you since you first got here. The moment I saw you twirling in the pasture, I had to hold myself back from getting too close. Not touching you has been driving me nuts. I have been so turned on, I can hardly do any work." He leaned in to whisper close to her lips. "And right now, I have this insane urge to see what your kiss is like, taste you, touch you, and breathe you."

Her eyes dilated so the blue was almost gone. Her lips parted, tempting him to bring his mouth down and lose himself in her. She brought her hands up to his chest, laying them on the surface. The heat of her touch burned through his shirt. The warmth tantalized him beyond anything he could do to stop where they were headed.

His voice came out in a low, husky tone. "If you don't stop me, Charlie, we're going there, right where I've been dying to be."

Her heartbeat fluttered in her throat, making him realize she was turned on to the point of combustion as well.

When she wet her lips with her tongue, he was lost. He couldn't stop himself if his life depended on it and right now if he didn't kiss her, he feared he would come apart at the seams.

He let his hands tangle in her hair at the base of her neck, his thumbs cradling her jawline. As their lips finally touched, he moaned deep in his throat. The jolt running through his body brought his heart to a thudding halt before it slammed against his ribs in a flat out chest beating rhythm. Her lips were like rose petals beneath his, soft and yielding.

She tilted her head to the side, aligning their mouths so he could deepen the kiss.

His world went white hot as need speared through him.

Her hands explored his chest, touching the surface in small discovering movements until they encircled his neck, and twisted in his hair.

He skimmed his hands down her back, over her hips, and cupped her ass bringing her in tight against his chest as he touched her lips with his tongue. He wanted to feel that connection with her, that all-consuming desire to be with one person. Charlie.

The globes of her butt were a perfect fit for his palms as she wrapped her legs around his waist. With her breasts flat against his chest, he could feel her nipples poking him even through his shirt. The sensation zinged through him like a bolt of lightning.

He trailed his lips over her cheek so he could reach her neck as he turned and placed her on the desktop. He ran his tongue up the side of the slim column until he reached her ear. "Your pleasure is mine."

His hand encircled her breast, toying with the nipple until it was a hard point. It wasn't enough. He wanted to feel her skin beneath his palm.

Grasping the bottom of her shirt in his fingers, he pulled the top over her head, leaving her only in her bra. The delicate edges were sexy lying against her skin. One finger traced the lace across the top of her breast. Goosebumps exploded over her flesh. "Gorgeous."

Her eyes were huge as she took in his face.

He yanked his t-shirt over his head, taking his hat with it, and tossing it onto a saddle nearby, not caring where it landed. "Are you sure about this?"

"No, but right now, I don't care. Nothing matters except this—you." She brought his head down so their lips met.

Her fingers worked the button at his waist, loosening it until it hung open and she could push the jeans down over his ass. He moaned deep in his throat when she touched his erection, the heat of her fingers scorching him even through his underwear.

He couldn't believe he was stiff already after getting himself off a few minutes before, but here he was rock hard and wanting to be inside her so badly he could taste it. "I need you."

"I've wanted this from the moment I saw you. It's wrong, so wrong, but it doesn't matter anymore." She pushed his jeans down off his butt until they slipped down his thighs to rest at the top of his boots.

He had a bad feeling she would regret this when it was all said and done.

Thoughts disappeared as she wrapped her hand around his cock, running her palm up and down his length. *Fuck, I'm going to die.* "Charlie, please. You're killing me."

Two fingers unbutton her pants at the waist before sliding along the elastic of her panties. Her belly jumped under his touch. He grabbed her jeans at the waist, dragging them and her underwear down over her hips in one strong tug. The pants snagged at her boots. He scooted backward enough to reach down and pull them off so he could tug her pants all the way off.

He hopped on one foot, trying desperately to get his own boot off.

A giggle escaped her lips as she rested back on her hands in nothing more than her bra. "Want some help?"

"I got it." He yanked the offending boots off and toed off the other one. He needed to get to his wallet for a condom.

Triumphantly holding up the foil package, he grinned as he took a seat on the rolling chair by the desk and positioned himself between her parted thighs.

When he ran his fingertip down the outside of her folds, she sucked in a ragged breath. "Nice." Her pussy was shaved except for a small patch of brown curls at the top of her mound. The lips already glistened with her juices. The heady scent of her arousal reached his nose, making his cock feel like it would explode at any minute if he didn't get inside her soon. "You are so wet."

He kissed her belly just below her belly button and ran his tongue down the center of her until he reached right above her clit.

A soft moan escaped her lips. She shivered beneath his hand.

She was so ready for this, he could hardly contain himself.

The tip of his tongue flicked over her clit before sliding up one side and down the other. He continued to tease her until her breathing came out in raspy pants of need.

"Please, Caleb."

Her hips lifted, bringing her pussy closer to his mouth. He slowed his movements, playfully licking her folds, the tip of her clit, the crease between her pussy and her thigh, and when he shoved two fingers into her hot channel and pressed down hard on her clit with his tongue, she came apart on a scream loud enough to shake the rafters of the barn.

A kiss to her inner thigh had her sighing.

He wanted to make her come again, but he couldn't wait to be inside her.

After he rolled the condom over his shaft, he stood up and positioned himself at her opening. He took her lips as he slowly pushed into her hot, tight pussy. *Holy fuck, she feels amazing.* He clamped his teeth together so tightly, he thought he might crack a tooth while he tried to hold still long enough to push his climax back down.

"Oh God, Caleb. Move. Please move."

Trying desperately to keep from coming, he thrust very deliberately. Her pussy quivered around him as she started breathing fast.

Her mouth fastened on his neck. She bit down on his skin before licking away the sting.

His world narrowed to the feeling of being inside her and how amazing it was to have her wetness surrounding him. He wasn't going to last long at this rate.

He brought his hand around to where they joined, slid his finger through the wetness created by their coupling, and brought it up and over her clit to rub it around and around her nub. He needed her to come before he did, otherwise this would be a wasted effort.

Her pussy contracted around him, signaling her climax was close. *Just a little more.* "Come for me, Charlie."

As she came apart on a scream of his name, he wasn't sure he could hold on. Nothing sounded sexier than the sound of a woman during a climax.

His own climax rumbled through him like thunder on the horizon during a massive storm. His balls drew up tight against his groin right before he lost control. Everything sheeted white and his gaze narrowed to nothing but the satisfaction in her eyes.

He shivered uncontrollably as he closed his eyes, trying to right his world.

Her fingers touched his chest, bringing his attention back to the woman in his arms. She was magnificent with her tousled hair, flushed skin, wet lips, and wide eyes. *Well fucked.*

When he slowly pulled out of her softness, they both groaned. He didn't like feeling like he was losing something precious. "I need to get rid of this." He pulled the latex from his softening cock and disposed of it in the trashcan.

She scooted her bottom off the desk, pulling up her underwear and jeans until she could button the material at the waist again.

Her fingers tangled in her hair, trying desperately to brush the knots from the strands.

He handed her the shirt she'd been wearing.

"Thanks."

"Sure."

Awkwardness seemed to shimmer in the small room as they both dressed. The heat that had been there before had cooled to a slow simmer.

Once they both had their clothes on, he touched her cheek with his fingertips before slipping his hand in her hair at the base of her neck and drawing her closer.

His lips brushed her. A moan rumbled in his chest at the taste of her mouth. If he wasn't careful, they'd be having sex again right there in the tack room.

When he finally lifted his head, he touched the corner of her mouth with his tongue. "You taste fantastic. I can't wait to have you beneath me again, this time in a real bed."

Her gaze dropped to the middle of his chest and when she lifted it again, he could see the confusion in her eyes. "We can't do this again, Caleb."

"Why the hell not?"

"It will make things weird, you working for me, if we're having sex."

He shook his head slightly and dropped his hand. Weird? She thought it would make things weird between them. Didn't she realize all she did was sign the checks? "You do know that although you own this place, I'm really the one in charge, right?"

* * * *

Charlie sputtered as if she was about to choke on her own spit. *He did not just say that.* "You aren't serious."

"Yeah. I mean you write the checks, pay the bills, buy the animals, but I'm the one running everything from out here. You're more of a figurehead at the helm. You know, captain of the ship and all except the crew runs everything from below."

She moved several steps away so she would throttle him with her hands. "Let's get something straight, Caleb. You work for me. Got it? Although you might think you run things around here, you don't. I am the money behind this operation. You are the labor."

The lines around his eyes deepened as he tried to hold his temper. She could see him flex his hands, clenching and unclenching his fists while he attempted to cool down. "It meant nothing that we just had sex?"

"No, it did not. We had sex. Big deal. Nothing changed. I am the boss. You are my foreman. I write your paycheck. If we were to have sex again, it would still be the same. I left a disastrous marriage not long ago, with a man who cheated on me with my best friend. I do not need another man in my life outside of those who work for me. If you think us having sex is going to change that dynamic, you're sorely mistaken."

His gaze fixed on her face for a moment before he pulled off his hat and ran his hand through his hair. "I find myself put in my place. I'm sorry. *Boss.*"

He pulled open the door to the tack room and walked out, leaving her standing in the center, not knowing what else to say or do.

What the hell just happened?

Her thoughts were jumbled. They'd had explosive sex, better than she'd ever had in the past, and now she stood there with her mouth in a firm line, watching him walk out of the barn doors, get into his truck, and speed down the driveway in a cloud of dust.

Would he be back? She didn't know and right now, she wasn't sure she cared. She had work to do.

The night sky looked brilliant as the sun disappeared behind the mountains in the distance. She'd already fed and watered the stallion, cleaned his stall, and made sure the tack room was tidy even though the images of the two of them having sex on the desk came back in sharp clarity.

Still no Caleb.

She sat on the porch sipping a glass of wine as she watched the road.

Still no Caleb.

The clock inside the house struck nine as she sighed and glanced down at the liquid in her glass. She might as well get used to the idea of finding a new foreman. He obviously wasn't coming back.

After she climbed to her feet, she pulled open the screen door and went inside. The silence surrounding her was deafening. The ticking of the old grandfather clock was the only sound.

I think I will take a nice hot shower and go to bed. I will need to be up early to feed the animals.

The door was locked with a twist of her hand on the deadbolt before she flipped off the porch light and headed toward her room. Once inside, she turned on the bedside lamp, grabbed her long t-shirt, and went to the bathroom.

Steam filled the room moments later as she stripped off her dirty clothes.

Hot water hit her skin, stinging like little needles pricking her everywhere. Her muscles began to relax under the spray. She really needed this after her day. Not that it had been all bad, but it had sure ended crappy.

As the water sluiced over her shoulders, she leaned back letting it wet her hair and massage her scalp. *Maybe I can wash away some of these thoughts.*

The mares would be arriving soon.

Amy would be starting work shortly.

She needed to get busy on the books.

The weather was real nice right now.

Caleb was gone.

Well hell. That didn't work very well.

Thoughts of Caleb bombarded her now that she'd let him in. He was one of the most capable men she knew. As a lover, he blew the doors off anyone she'd been with before, making her feel things she shouldn't, and realizing what she'd been missing in the past. The way his eyes crinkled when he smiled. How hard his chest was beneath her palms when they'd had sex in the tack room. His scent—musky, sweaty, manly smell. The firmness of his lips when he'd kissed her—no bombarded her senses when his mouth had taken hers. How sure his hands were as he skimmed them over her body, learning every spot that turned her on.

Need simmered beneath the surface of her skin as she played over them making love in her mind.

If he hadn't been such an idiot, maybe they could have worked something out.

No, I told him it wouldn't happen again. It shouldn't have happened to begin with. Having sex with an employee is all kinds of wrong.

He was becoming more than an employee.

She shut off the water in the shower, dried herself off, and then slipped on her pajamas. Hopefully, sleep would come, although she didn't know if her dreams would be invaded with images and feelings she didn't want to face.

The sheets were cool against her skin when she slipped beneath them to settle in for the night. The lamp on the nightstand reflected images on the ceiling over her head as she let her thoughts jumble.

Things she'd thought she had under control really weren't. Her feelings were tied up in knots and she didn't know which way to turn. She wanted Caleb here, but did she want a relationship with him beyond employee and employer?

She rolled over and punched her pillow before settling down and flipping off the light. Moonlight streamed through the gauzy curtains, cutting a white path across her bedroom floor.

Her lips tingled from the memory of his kiss.

Her body hummed as she thought about his hands on her skin.

Her heart thumped in her chest when she realized yes, she did want him in her life beyond just being her foreman.

Now, how did she go about getting him back to the ranch without looking like an idiot?

Chapter Eight

Caleb slumped over the beer mug between his fingers, staring into the yellowish liquid. Music swirled around him. The bar was busy tonight. People moved in waves from one side to the other as the men were checking out the women and vice versa.

He'd come to the bar intent on finding some alcohol, a willing woman, and a soft bed for the night. The same beer sat in front of him that he'd started with several hours before. Several women had approached him, but after he'd had a chance to look into their eyes, he realized he didn't want them. He wanted the stubborn blue-eyed beauty who'd twisted his guts into knots. *Damn her anyway.*

Why couldn't he just forget her and move on? She obviously didn't see things the way he did when it came to running the ranch. Her ranch. *Well fuck.* As much as he didn't want to admit it, that particular parcel of land did belong to her. She'd paid for it lock, stock, and barrel. Why he found it so hard to remember she was his boss, he didn't know.

One finger traced the condensation on his glass.

A hand came down on his shoulder.

He looked up to find his brother Cameron looming behind him.

"You look like hell, Caleb."

"Yeah, I bet I do."

Cameron took the stool next to him, signaling the bartender for a drink. "Beer."

The bartender was a nice looking woman in her own right, but he couldn't help but compare her to Charlie's soft curves and pretty smile. *Damn, I have it bad.*

His brother turned to him and bumped him in the shoulder. "So what's got you some down in the dumps?"

"Nothin'."

"A woman, huh?"

"What gave you that idea?" he asked, turning to look at his brother. Cameron was as light as he was dark. They'd often laughed as they grew up comparing their coloring and teasing each other about who was adopted in the family.

"Because you are the man who swore he would never get caught up with anyone." He took a sip of his beer then set it back down on the napkin. "I have been watching you for the last hour from the other side of the bar and you've barely drunk any of that beer. It's not like you. You've been approached by several nice looking females and you've not even taken a second glance. My only conclusion is a woman."

Caleb went back to staring at his beer before he brought it to his lips and took a drink. The beer wasn't even cold anymore.

The two of them sat in silence for a moment.

"How's the job?"

"I'm unemployed."

"I thought you were working out at that ranch outside of town?"

"I was until today."

"You get fired?"

"Nope. I quit."

"You said it was a lucrative job. Good pay. Nice place training horses for some city-slicker who wanted to see if they could make a few bucks."

"It was."

"Why'd you quit then?"

Caleb turned to look right into Cameron's eyes. "Because I fucked my boss."

Cameron threw back his head a laughed so loud, people around them stopped and looked. "You didn't."

"Yes, I did."

"And?"

He turned back to stare into his beer. "I stuck my foot in my mouth when she said it couldn't or wouldn't happen again."

"What did you say?"

"I said something to the effect that 'she only wrote the checks. I ran the place from the barn.'"

"You are fucking stupid, Caleb."

"Don't you think I know that?"

"What are you going to do about it?"

"I don't know." He took another drink before pushing the now warm beer away. "It's not that I need the job. I really don't, but if I walk away, I have a feeling I'll be making the biggest mistake of my life."

"I never thought I'd hear something like that come from your mouth."

"Well, it has." He glanced at the mirror behind the bar, watching as people moved behind him. A woman walked up next to his right shoulder. He did a double take as he looked closer. Hair color was the same as Charlie's, but when she looked up and caught his gaze in the mirror, he realized it wasn't her. "I need to find another job, something that won't get me into trouble."

"If you don't need the money, why don't you take a few weeks off before you find something else? You are a talented trainer. You should be able to find something quick enough."

Caleb shrugged before signaling the bartender for another beer.

"So what is so special about her?"

It took a moment for Caleb to realize he could describe her in one word. Amazing.

* * * *

The gelding her father had sent from his place arrived a few days after Caleb had disappeared and not come back. The animal was stabled on the other end of the barn from the stallion to keep the peace.

Charlie stood outside his stall watching him munch on some hay. The solid paint with four white feet had always been her favorite. He'd already started training, but she needed to get him finished up. Amy would be working with him in the morning.

With her head leaning against the metal bars along the side of the half-door, she closed her eyes and sighed. The ranch had been way too quiet and lonely.

Her days were spent cleaning stalls, doing some of the repairs she could do, and feeding the animals. The weather had been gorgeous, but sitting outside on the patio with a glass of wine, watching the sun go down had become her nightly ritual. Night sounds would lull her to sleep. Her dreams were tangled up with images of Caleb and how he'd made love to her.

During the evenings, she would make her dinner and sit alone at the dining room table as she picked at her food.

The silence was deafening.

Amy had turned into a pretty good friend. They'd spent some time together in the house watching chick-flicks, eating popcorn, and gossiping. Charlie wanted to ask her about Caleb, but the topic never came up. Amy hadn't mentioned the fact that he wasn't there either, even though Charlie assumed she'd been curious. It had been a big deal to know they were okay working together and now he was gone.

He'd been gone a week and it seemed like a lifetime.

She opened her eyes to find the gelding standing almost nose-to-nose with her. "This is dumb. If he doesn't want to be here, I can't make him, and it's obvious he doesn't want to." The blaze on the gelding's nose was soft under her hand. "Oh, Champ. What have I gotten myself into, huh?"

The pop and crunch of gravel under a vehicle brought her attention to the doors of the barn. *There shouldn't be anyone coming to the house this time of day.*

The slam of a door had her tilting her head as she moved slowly toward the tack room. If she had to, there was a crowbar sitting on the desk inside where she'd kept it ever since Caleb had left. Being alone on the ranch, wasn't a good idea.

A silhouette of a man appeared in the doorway.

"Can I help you?" she called out.

He didn't say anything, just moved in her direction with a sure step until he stood in front of her.

Caleb.

He backed her up against the door, using his knee to spread her thighs. The hardness of his muscles bit into her clit, driving a moan into her throat.

One hand grabbed her wrists, forcing them over her head as he leaned closer.

His fingers brushed the hair from her forehead so gently she wanted to cry.

Callused fingertips skimmed along her jaw until he reached her chin, bringing her face up until his gaze locked with hers.

She couldn't read the expression in his eyes, but the intensity of it had her breath coming out choppy and strained. *Desire? Need? He looks like he wants to eat me alive.*

He leaned closer until she could feel every exhale on her lips, warm and moist like the air before a storm. Still, he waited.

The solid expanse of his chest pinned her to the boards biting into her back. She didn't care. He was here.

Time slipped by.

The gelding whinnied in his stall.

Still, he didn't move closer.

She licked her lips as she parted them on a sigh. Not knowing what he planned to do, her body hummed with anticipation, the kind that had her on edge right before something amazing was about to happen.

He waited.

Unable to hold his gaze any longer and dying to have his mouth on hers, she slowly closed her eyes.

The brief touch of his mouth was her undoing, the soft brush of his lips, nothing more, almost as if he whispered an endearment against her lips.

She held her breath.

He touched his tongue to her bottom lip, slipping it gently over the surface, until she opened for him, wanting everything from this man.

Their tongues danced, each sliding over the other until they were both breathless. He continued to devour her until she hurt from the need to have him touch her, something…anything.

The moment his hand found her breast, kneading the soft flesh with his fingers, she almost lost control right there riding his thigh. *More. I need more.*

Needing air, she tore her mouth from his only to have him move across her cheek and down her neck, biting the flesh beneath his mouth until he grasped the edge of her shirt. He reached the first button and glanced up before grabbing it with his teeth and popping it loose. His tongue followed the revealed skin to the second button. Again, he removed it with his teeth.

He continued down the front of her blouse, eliminating each one until her shirt hung open.

With his hands no longer holding hers, she held on to his shoulders as her head laid back against the wall behind her.

His tongue circled her belly button before kissing the skin and then moving back up toward her breasts. He pushed her bra out of his way as his left palm rasped over her straining nipple and his mouth encircled the other.

Words escaped her. She could do nothing but moan while the sensations bombarded her body so fast, she could barely process them.

No words passed between them as he scooped her up, wrapping her legs around his waist and headed for the house.

When his boots hit the porch with a clump, her brain clicked on. "Caleb, no. Wait." She struggled in his arms until he let her go and she could step back. Her back hit the doorframe as she placed her hand on his chest while she struggled to bring her bra back into place.

"What?"

"We shouldn't do this, not until we've talked. This is what got us in a fight before and we need to clear the air about a few things."

His jaw tightened as he exhaled on a rush. It took a moment for his gaze to return to hers. "All right." He brought her shirt back together. "Sorry about the buttons."

She couldn't help but grin. "No, you're not." A quick tie of the ends secured it below her breasts. "Besides, it was damn sexy." She reached for his hand and tugged him through the doorway with her.

They reached the kitchen a moment later as she gently pushed him into a chair at the table. "Something to drink? Coffee, tea, milk, soda, or beer?"

"Nothing, thanks."

Needing something to do with her hands, she grabbed a sponge from the sink and began wiping the nonexistent dirt from the countertop. She needed to say something, but she wasn't sure what. The conversation they'd had before seemed almost a distant memory. A difficult one, no less. She couldn't let him get away with his attitude about who actually ran this ranch. If he thought he was the only one who could make decisions about what went on around here, he was sorely mistaken. Then again, she needed him and his expertise to make things ran smoothly. How did a physical relationship between them fit into the scheme of things? She certainly was not ready for anything beyond that.

His hands came down on her shoulders and she jumped. She hadn't heard him move with how tangled up her thoughts were. The heat from his palms did nothing to calm her racing heart.

His lips brushed the top of her head as he pulled her back against his chest. "I'm sorry about what happened before, Charlie. I don't know what was going through my head. Maybe I was feeling out of control, which is a constant state with you around. I'm a man used to having everything my way or nothing."

He slowly turned her to face him. The confusion in his gaze melted her heart. She knew what it was like to battle for everything you had. Whether he knew that same kind of fight, she didn't know, but he had to figure out how to let her do this, otherwise, there would be nothing for them to do but walk away. "I too am used to being the one in charge. This is going to be a constant point of contention between us, I'm afraid, unless we figure out how to compromise."

His fingers were rough and hard against her skin as he pushed her hair back away from her face and tucked it behind her ear. "It's not easy for me." His voice whispered over her lips in a warm caress.

"I'm sure it's not, but you have to understand, you are not the one losing everything if this goes belly up. I am. It's all or nothing for me, Caleb. There is no going back on this."

"I'll do my best to give you the reins, darlin', in the barn, but in the bedroom, you give them back to me."

Her skin tingled as she looked deep into his eyes. She liked a man to take control between the sheets, and the thought of letting Caleb do whatever he wanted to her, had her pussy dampening and her nipples pebbling hard.

His fingers scraped along the edge of her neck until his hand cupped the back of her head. A sexy little smile lifted the corners of his mouth as he glanced down at her breasts before coming back up to her eyes. "Is that a yes?"

"Yes," she breathed, tipping her head back to give him access to everything he wanted.

He nudged her ear with his nose, pushing her hair aside so he could skim his lips down her throat.

They took a step back together, bringing her ass against the edge of the counter. He lifted her and set her on the top, leaving her almost eye level with him.

"You are so gorgeous. I can't get enough of you."

Her hands shook as she reached for the ends of her shirt and untied it, parting the material to reveal her breasts.

He took the shirt at the shoulders and peeled it down her arms, his gaze following the path as it pooled at her waist.

She wanted him to touch her, caress her flesh until she moaned his name out loud. She swept the hat from his head, leaving it lying on the counter before she plowed her fingers through his dark hair and forcing his lips against hers. His taste was intoxicating, all male and so luscious.

His tongue swept inside her mouth, rubbing along hers, first one side then the other. She couldn't breathe without taking in his scent, his unique smell that she only associated with Caleb.

He brought both hands up to cup her face as he pulled his mouth from hers. "Are you sure about this, Charlie? I don't want to do anything to mess this up."

"I'm sure. I've been going crazy without you here. It's been all me and I don't like it one bit. It's been lonely and miserable." She kissed the corner of his lips. "Make me forget that loneliness."

He swept her up in his arms in the same position they came to the house in, her legs wrapped around his waist as he headed down the hall.

The moment they crossed the threshold, he kicked the door closed and then deposited her on her feet at the edge of the bed. The last time they'd been in this room together, she'd been so sick she couldn't see. This time would be different. This time she wanted him here in her bed, in her life, and a part of whatever the future held for her ranch.

The rest would work itself out in time. She hoped.

Heat blazed in his eyes as he slowly peeled the straps of her bra down off her shoulders, taking the cups off her breasts and revealing her flesh to his gaze. His hands skimmed down her arms, forcing her to keep them at her sides when she would have reached for him. "Stay just like that."

He bent down until he could encircle her breast with his mouth, tonguing the nipple on the right as he palmed the left.

Her body vibrated with the need to touch him, but he wasn't about to let her. The restraint wasn't necessarily physical as it was mental. He didn't want her to move and she wasn't going to if she could help it.

Her skin broke out in goose bumps when he licked around her areola. The sensations he was causing bombarded her senses to overload. Her panties were so damp, she shifted her weight to put a little friction against her clit in a vain effort to relieve some of the pressure building inside her.

"Naughty girl. Do you want me to touch you?"

A moan escaped her lips as she breathlessly sighed, "Yes."

Two of his fingers worked the button loose at her waist, parting her jeans so he could slide his hand beneath the waistband of her panties. The moment his fingers touched her clit, she jumped slightly at the feeling.

"So wet and so needy, but I'm not ready to slide into that hot little pussy yet. Nope. I'm going to taste you until you are begging me for release." He grabbed her pants at the waist, pushing them down until they hung up at the top of her boots. After he glanced up to catch her gaze with his, he gently pushed her down on the edge of the bed, pulled her boots off, and then removed her jeans the rest of the way, leaving her panties in place.

Not sure what he planned, she leaned up on her elbows to watch.

One finger ran down the elastic between her thigh and her pussy, and her vagina clenched in anticipation. She wanted him to touch her, lick her, and be inside her with everything she had. He placed his mouth against her clit on the outside of her panties, licking until the material was soaked. "I can smell your arousal."

"I want you."

A cocky little grin spread across his lips. "You'll have me in due time, but first I am going to make you so horny your eyes roll back in your head and you come the moment I get inside you."

She laid back on the bed with her arms above her head—waiting to see what he would do next.

He hooked his finger in the edges of her panties, slipping them down off her hips and legs until she lay bare before him like some sacrifice to the Gods.

His lips slipped up the inside of her leg until she could feel his breath ruffling the curls of her pussy. Everything held as she waited for the touch of his tongue where she wanted it the most. He didn't disappoint.

The moment he touched her clit, her world narrowed to the feeling of his mouth on her. Rubbing his tongue firmly up one side and then the other, he had her on edge in moments. She grasped the bedding in her hands, trying desperately for that one small touch that would send her over the top.

His tongue moved to a different spot. She wanted to scream as he took her up again, slow enough her legs were shaking as she tried to reach for climax.

He slowly licked her from vagina up and over her clit and then back down in a movement meant to drive her nuts. Her breath came out so fast and hard she thought she would pass out from lack of oxygen.

Still, he tormented her with pleasure, touching, licking, and making her want him bad enough she wanted to scream at the top of her lungs. She whimpered before she began to beg. "Please, Caleb. God, make me come, please."

He kissed the inside of her thigh before standing up, rolling on a condom he'd pulled from Lord knows where, and slammed inside her in one thrust.

A climax broke over her in a rush, crashing through her body like waves against a jagged shore as she came screaming his name.

"Very nice, love, but I think there is more where that came from."

She looked at him through half-closed eyelids. "When did you lose your clothes in that mix of sensations you were bombarding me with?"

"I'm crafty like that."

"Indeed."

"No more talk. Moans, groans, and screams are permitted only." His thrusts began again in a rapid, body-pounding rhythm.

Her body lit up again as he continued to thrust, driving into her with such force he had to place one hand on her hip to hold her in place. The other hand came around between them to rub her clit in time with his rhythm. His cock filled places she'd never known existed, sliding over spots she didn't know made her even want him more.

When he grabbed her legs and pushed her knees higher near her shoulders, it brought her pelvis up and opened her to his every pounding slide.

His cock hit a place behind her pelvic bone that shot her straight to oh-my-god arousal and sent her crashing over into a mind-blowing orgasm so fast, she didn't know what hit her.

Sweat dripped down his temple, sliding down his neck and chest. His eyes were closed in concentration as he tried to hold back his own climax. His breath came out in a halting, disjointed effort to breathe until it all stopped for that split second as his orgasm washed over him.

He was magnificent when he came and it was a sight she would never get tired of seeing. For her, it meant she'd done something right for the man in her life.

Chapter Nine

Caleb traced his fingers down Charlie's arm where it lay across his chest. Her soft snores and warm breath on his skin made him smile. It wasn't very often he spent time with a woman after having sex. He usually grabbed his clothes and beat a path to the door, smiling and waving on his way out. Right now, he had no intention of going anywhere. He liked having her draped over him, her thigh against his, her feet wrapped up with his at the bottom of the bed, and her skin next to his.

He could get used to making love with her regularly. They were well matched in the sack, which seemed to be unusual for him. Normally, he gave more than he received. It was just the way he operated. For him, it was all about the woman and making her feel good, but with Charlie, he got a lot out of their time together. Their personalities clashed a little though. He'd have to work on that part if he wanted to stay here for any length of time. He needed to get over the superiority thing with her. She was the boss and he needed to remember that even if they were sleeping together.

Her snores stopped as she tipped her head back on his shoulder. With her hair in a wild disarray from making love, she looked gorgeous. Her eyes were bright and sparkling as she looked up at him. "Hey."

"Hi."

"What time is it?"

"Six, I think."

"Wow. I slept for quite a long time. I guess I was tired." She leaned in a brushed a kiss across his lips. "Hungry?"

"Yeah, kind of."

"Let's grab a shower and then I'll fix something for supper." She sat up and tossed her legs over the side of the bed before she pushed her hair over her shoulder.

Unable to help himself, he reached out and ran his fingers through the strands hanging down her back. He loved to touch her hair. It was so soft and wild.

She glanced back with a smile as she stood up and went to grab some clean clothes. "Care to join me?"

"A naked woman with water running over her breasts, soap slicked skin, and a smile like that? How could I refuse?" He climbed from the bed and then followed her into the bathroom.

The moment she turned on the shower, steam filled the room, fogging up the mirror he was using to watch her naked ass. She had to be one of the most beautiful women he'd ever seen and he couldn't get over the fact that he was having sex with her on what he hoped would be a regular basis.

They needed to talk a few things out to make sure they were on the same page with things on the ranch. He would be careful how he worded things with her, so she wouldn't feel like he was trying to take over. Her money was on the line, not his.

Charlie held out her hand, dragging him into the shower stall with her as she grabbed the soap and began to wash his chest. He loved the feeling of her hands on his skin, smoothing themselves over the ridges of his abdomen, down between his legs, around his balls, and back up his chest. "Good Lord, woman, you are going to kill me."

When the soap had been washed away, she dropped to her knees in front of him and took his cock between her luscious lips. "Oh God." His voice was barely a whisper as she licked up the front, following the veins on his cock around to the back. Her fingers rolled his balls, making them ache to come. *Not yet.* "If you don't stop, Charlie, I'm gonna come in your mouth."

She hummed deep in her throat as she continued to lick, suck, and slide her hand up and down in conjunction with the movement of her mouth.

Unable to hold back his orgasm, he moaned as he leaned back against the cold tile of the shower. Both of his hands were fisted in her hair as she ran her tongue under the head of his cock. He lost it, shooting his load into the back of her throat. His legs felt like jelly while he tried to bring his breathing under control. Charlie continued to slowly lick his softening cock until he was completely flaccid.

Now it was his turn to make her lose it.

He grabbed the loofa in his hands, soaping it up well before he began to slowly slide it over her breasts.

When she lifted her hands to grab his wrists, he said, "Hands at your sides. Don't move them again."

Her eyes cracked open as she stared at him for a moment before closing them again and returning her hands to her sides.

"Good girl."

Her nipples looked painfully hard as he ran the scratchy material of the loofa over them. Soap dribbled down her skin, sliding in a long trail until it reached the top of the curls at the juncture of her thighs. She tipped her head back as a soft moan escaped her lips. Water sluiced over her shoulders taking the soap further down her body.

Goosebumps popped up on her arms when his mouth closed over her right nipple. He could only imagine the conflict going on inside her as she tried to process the sensations and not move at the same time.

He slipped a hand between her thighs, touching the hard little nub trying to hide behind the hood.

Her hot breath fanned over his ear while he continued to tongue her nipple. She trembled beneath his mouth.

"Please."

He hummed against her flesh, enjoying the hard nub as he rubbed it with his tongue.

"Caleb, please. I need to come so badly."

He moved his hand around to the top of her buttocks before sliding down the crack and fingering her ass hole with his index finger. She sucked in a ragged breath as he pushed one finger inside.

When he lifted his head, he could see the fight going on within her. She enjoyed the forbidden touch, but she obviously hadn't had any experience with anal sex. He would have to remedy that in the future.

"Easy, darlin'. We won't go there tonight."

The tension around her mouth eased before lifting her lips in a small smile.

He lifted her leg, wrapping it around his hip as he lifted her so she was open to his thrust. "Shit. I don't have a condom in here."

"I'm clean and on the pill."

"I was tested less than three months ago."

"I'm okay with it if you are."

"I would love to go bare inside you so I can feel every bit of you as I slide deep."

She cupped his face with her hands. "Make love to me, Caleb."

Unable to hold himself back any longer, he thrust balls deep inside her. A gasp escaped her lips before a throaty moan echoed in the steamy shower.

"Yes. That's it. Right there."

The feeling of her wrapped around him had him on the edge of climax in moments, but he wouldn't leave her behind. She would come hard if he had anything to say about it. "Hold onto my shoulders."

He put both hands on her hips, lifting her as he pounded into her. His thrusts drove his cock so deep inside her that he swore his balls were about to explode.

Her groans of pleasure were his undoing.

The moment her mouth latched onto his neck, sucking the skin between her lips, he thought for sure he wouldn't be able to stop his climax. "Charlie. Slide your hand between us and play with your clit."

The uncertainty in her gaze was almost his undoing.

When he felt her hand slide down his abdomen, he smiled.

The moment her eyes slipped closed as her fingers worked her clit, he knew he wouldn't be able to keep his heart from getting involved with this woman. She would be his downfall.

* * * *

Embarrassment flushed her cheeks when she heard Caleb's words. He wanted her to make herself come. Not that she'd never done it before, but it was usually in the privacy of her room where she could lose herself in the moment with the fantasy of some unknown man.

This was Caleb and he wanted her to orgasm.

When her fingers touched her clit, she felt herself climb the hill straight out onto the ledge of an orgasm that would blow her mind.

Caleb pounded into her in a rhythm meant to bring them both to climax. The tip of his cock hit that sweet spot inside her that made her belly quiver and her heart race. His thrusts became disjointed as he braced one hand on the shower tile behind her.

"Come for me, Charlie. I want you to squeeze me so tight you might break me in half."

He slammed into her, lifting her and fucking her until she couldn't breathe. His mouth latched onto her neck, biting a small bit of skin to the point of pain, and throwing her into a climax that had her seeing stars. "Caleb!"

Her body shuddered as he finally pounded into her for the last time and came with a sigh of her name on his lips. The moment his cock slipped out of her, he released her legs, letting them slowly slide down his body.

The water started to turn cold, so they rinsed quickly before she turned the knob, shutting it off. He reached over and grabbed a towel, drying her off from her shoulders to her toes. The grin remaining on his lips made her want to kiss him all over again. Instead, she dried him off, lingering on his cock and balls a little longer than she needed to. He didn't stop her though. In fact, he got aroused again, his cock becoming long and firm as she dried him thoroughly.

Folding the towel over the rack, she grabbed his hand leading him back into her bedroom. "We should get dressed and get something to eat."

"I know what I want, but that won't fill my belly."

She felt the trickle of desire dampen her pussy. Would she ever get enough of him? She doubted it. They probably needed to slow things down a bit. Spending all the time between the sheets was great in a fantasy world, but they lived in real time and she had a ranch to run. "As much as I would love to make love with you again, I think we should get some food. I have some paperwork to do this evening."

One eyebrow sprung up over his right eye.

She ran a finger down his chest. "Of course, that doesn't mean things can't heat up later on."

"My thoughts exactly, darlin'."

He reached down to the pile of clothes on the floor and grabbed his boxer-briefs before pulling them and his jeans over his scrumptious butt. The man had everything. Nice chest, gorgeous ass, an abdomen to die for, and when he looked her with those eyes, she would do anything he asked.

With his butt firmly planted on the edge of her bed, he watched intently as she brought her t-shirt over her head, leaving her bra off. Knowing she had no intention of going anywhere tonight other than back between the sheets with him, she slipped on a pair of running shorts and her slippers.

A grin lifted the corners of his mouth when he looked at her feet. "I love those."

She glanced down at her Eeyore slippers. "They are comfortable."

"I can imagine."

"Come on. Let's get some food."

He followed her down the hall to the kitchen where she grabbed some things out of the refrigerator to whip up something to eat. She was usually pretty good at throwing together a meal from little to nothing. Tonight would be pasta with some chicken, spinach, and Alfredo sauce.

The scrape of the chair leg on the floor told her he'd taken a seat at the table.

"Would you like a beer or a glass of wine?"

"Sure. A beer would be great."

While the chicken sizzled in the pan, she grabbed a bottle from the fridge and took it to him. The sight of him sitting at her table with nothing but a pair of low-slung jeans riding his hips had her mouth watering to taste him. She hummed her appreciation as she licked her lips.

"You need to quit lookin' at me like that, darlin'."

"Why is that?"

"Because if you don't, I'm gonna take you right here on this table and to hell with supper."

Her heart pounded in her chest as her body shivered in delight. The thought of him being all dominant and demanding made her want him even more. If he were to take what he wanted, right here and right now, she might just fall in love with him. She would have to be careful with those thoughts. Falling in love with her foreman was such a bad idea on all fronts, including keeping her heart intact.

He pulled her between his thighs, trapping her in place as he ran his hands up her legs. Calluses abraded deliciously against her skin. She cupped his face before bringing her mouth down to his. The feel of his lips under hers had her shifting her stance to bring some relief to her throbbing clit.

His fingers slipped under the edge of her shorts and right against her pussy, making her want to melt into his arms and never leave.

Her breathing sped up, forcing her breasts to rise and fall. "The chicken is going to burn," she whispered against his lips. Stepping back out of his reach, she grinned at the look on his face. He was definitely wound up if the bulge behind his jeans was any kind of indicator.

"Tease."

"Hmm. Maybe just a little, but no worries. I'll take care of you after we eat."

"I want to eat, but it's not chicken."

She turned back to the stove and finished cooking the chicken before adding the Alfredo sauce and spinach. The noodles bubbled in another pan on the stove while she stirred them to keep them from sticking together. Keeping her eyes on the food came with a price. Her imagination went wild thinking about him sitting behind her watching her move around the kitchen. She dared not look at him, otherwise, she would lose her concentration for sure.

Caleb pressed a kiss against her bare neck. "I'm going to go check on the stallion while supper is cooking."

"Check on the gelding as well. He arrived the other day," she said, turning to face him as she looped her arms around his neck for a moment.

"Is that the one Amy is working with?"

"It is. She hasn't started with him yet. She'll be here in the morning bright and early."

"Do you have any other prospects coming in for training?"

"Yes. I have two clients that have booked sessions. They'll be here tomorrow as well."

"Perfect. I can work with one." His lips brushed hers briefly. "We need to find at least one more trainer."

"I know, but I haven't had much luck."

"I'll make some phone calls tomorrow. We don't want to keep your clients waiting for a trainer."

"You would do that?"

"Of course, Charlie. You hired me as your foreman. It's part of my job." He placed a kiss on her nose and stepped back. "Be right back."

Her gaze fixed on his incredibly sexy ass as he headed for the front door. When he disappeared through it, closing it softly behind him, she let her thoughts drift to his statement about calling some people. She didn't want him to do it because it was his job, she wanted him to do it because he cared about her and the ranch. *I can't have it both ways. Either he wants me for me or he wants the ranch because he is being paid to be here.*

"Well shit. This is a screwed up scenario if I've ever seen one."

Her cell phone jangled on the table where she'd laid it earlier.

"Hey, Dad. What's up?"

"I wanted to see how the gelding was doing."

"He's fine. One of my trainers is going to start him tomorrow and see how well he's retained what we've done before. I'm sure he'll do fine."

"He's a smart horse. I'm sure there won't be much he'll need a refresher on. How about the stallion you bought?"

"Raring to go once the mares get here."

"When are they due in?"

"Late tomorrow."

"How is everything else going?"

"Good. I have two clients who will be bringing their prospects to us tomorrow to start. They are paying very well for the services. I just hope we can live up to their expectations."

"I'm sure you'll do fine. You know your stuff, baby girl. Keep an eye on your trainers and everything will work out."

"I plan to. Amy is working with the gelding first. I'll be watching her tomorrow to see how she does, and Caleb is taking on one of the new animals when they get settled."

"Sounds like you've got a good plan in motion. Watch your budget though. Expenses can get out of hand quickly."

"I have it under control, Dad. Don't worry."

"You are my baby. Of course I worry and you know if you need some money, don't hesitate to call me."

She rolled her eyes as she leaned against the countertop. "I will, but you know I have to do this on my own."

"Yes, I know. Think of it as your inheritance."

"Since I sure don't want to think about you dying, I won't go there with that."

A deep rumbling laugh met her ear. "I'm not going anywhere, sweetheart, but I do tend to invest in my kids."

"I love you."

"I love you too, sweetie. I'll talk to you later. My phone is beeping there is another call and it looks like it's my buddy Phil. I'll call you later this week."

"Okay. Talk to you later."

"Bye."

The screen door banged as Caleb came back inside the house just as she was putting the plates of food on the table. She looked up as he came into the kitchen. "What's wrong?"

"There is a problem."

Chapter Ten

"Problem?"

Caleb didn't want to tell her. She probably wouldn't take it well, but he had to. It was his job to run the ranch and this would set her back enough that it could cause her to lose the place. He ran his fingers through his hair. This wasn't going to be easy. "It's the stallion. We need to get the vet out here right now."

Her eyes widened at his words. "What's wrong with him?"

"I think he's got colic. He hasn't shit since day before yesterday in his stall, he's sweating, and he's rolling."

Colic wasn't anything to mess with. "I'll call right now." She grabbed her cell phone. "I don't know the local vet."

He took her phone and dialed. "Doc Millard? Hey, it's Caleb Armstrong. Yeah, hi. Listen, I am out here at Charlie Abrams' place. Yeah, you know the place. She has a stallion out here that I think he's turning colicky. He's got some of the symptoms. Can you come out and look at him? Thanks, Doc. I appreciate it. See you in a few." He clicked the phone off and handed it back to her. "He'll be here in about fifteen minutes."

She sagged against the counter. "I guess I should go out and look at him," she said, straightening again. "Let me put on some jeans and boots and I'll be right there."

Caleb nodded as he headed back out the door. He should check on the gelding too since he was their responsibility as well. The light from inside the barn lit the way for him as he made his way through the double doors. When he peeked in on the gelding, he appeared completely normal as he stood in the corner eating his hay.

The stallion paced in his stall from what he could see from near the door. Another indicator something wasn't right. It was going to be a long night, he feared. They would have to take turns walking him and trying to keep him moving so he could pass whatever blockage he had in his gut. Colic was painful for an animal and it wasn't something he'd wish on anyone.

When he approached the stallion's stall, he looked at him with sad eyes as if to say, help me. He knew the animal had to be uncomfortable.

The stallion's halter hung on the nail next to the sliding door, so he slipped it over his head and secured it behind his ears before grabbing a rope. "Let's get some exercise big guy." Caleb led him out to the arena and they began to walk around and around the enclosure. Unsure of what else to do, Caleb began to talk about everything, his childhood, his parents, his horse training, and his relationship with Charlie. "You know, boy, I'm not sure what to think of her. She's smart, funny, sexy as hell, and when we come together it's like fireworks, you know? I'd really like to get to know her more, but I'm not sure that's a good idea. She is my boss after all." He gathered the reins in his hands, sliding the polyester rope across his palm as they walked. "You sure have the life, boy. Girl's whenever you want them just back up their ass to you and you hop on. No wooing involved." The stallion tossed his head in agreement and Caleb laughed. He felt kind of stupid talking to the horse, but somehow hearing everything out loud made it a little more plausible.

The sound of an engine coming up the drive brought his attention back to the arena. *Must be the vet.* Headlights illuminated the side of the barn for a moment before flicking off. Boots crunched on the gravel as someone approached. "Caleb?"

"In here, Doc." Caleb led the stallion to the fenced off area. "Nice to see you although I wish it was under different circumstances."

"Me too, son." Doc Millburn climbed through the railing, approaching the stallion on the right while he ran his hands over his side. "How's he doing?"

"He's been okay while we walked, but in his stall, he was pacing, nipping at his flanks, and rolling."

"Appears to be sweating too."

"I noticed that."

The vet felt along the horse's belly. "He does seem to be a bit bloated." His stethoscope in hand, Doc Millburn listened for abdominal sounds. "I don't hear much. You are probably right in saying it is colic, Caleb. I'll give him something for pain. You know the drill. Keep him away from food. Keep him walking without tiring him out too much but prevent him from rolling. I'll be back in the morning to see how he's doing."

"Thanks, Doc."

Charlie came skidding to a halt next to the fence. "Caleb?"

"Doc, this is Charlie. She owns the place. Charlie, this is Doc Millburn, our local vet."

"Charlie, huh? Cute."

"Yeah, my dad thought so."

"Your dad wouldn't be Charlie Abrams would he?"

"That's him."

"Wow. I've known Charlie for a lot of years. I worked the circuit for a long time before my wife insisted I stay home and retire." He waved his hand. "As you can see, not so much for retirement, but I'm home more or it appears that way." He laughed. "Nice to meet you, ma'am." He tipped his hat. "Your stallion has colic. I've given Caleb instructions and I'm sure he can relay them to you. The basics is all, and I'm sure he'll be fine in a few days. Watch for droppings to make sure he's going." Doc Millburn worked his way between the fence rails. "Tell your pop hi for me. I'll have to call him some time."

"I'm sure he'd enjoy that."

"I'll come by in the morning to check on your boy there."

"I appreciate you coming by."

"No problem. I've known Caleb a long time, if he thinks I need to see an animal then I come."

"I'll keep that in mind for the future."

Doc Millburn looked between the two of them as she moved closer to where Caleb stood with the horse. "Ah. I see. Well then, I hope ya'll are happy."

She blushed as she ran her hand over the stallion's rump.

"I'll see you in the mornin'."

"Thanks again."

"You're welcome."

Doc whistled as he walked back out the barn doors to his truck. Caleb heard the beast turn over right before the sound faded as he drove down the driveway. When he glanced at Charlie, she appeared to be studying the dust on the tips of her boots. "I guess it's going to be a long night of watching him."

"Yeah, I guess so," she said as her gaze met his.

"I've been walking him some and I don't think we need to do it continuously, but we'll need to watch him tonight to make sure he doesn't lay down and roll. If he twists his gut, we'll be in trouble."

She blew out a breath that forced her bangs from her forehead. "You go on home, Caleb. He's my responsibility. I'll stay with him tonight and you can watch him tomorrow."

Knowing it was just as much his responsibility as it was hers, he shook his head. "I'll take my turn tonight. You can sleep and then be here when Doc comes in the morning."

"This is crazy, Caleb. It is my place to take care of him."

The warmth of her hand on his arm sent shivers racing up until they exploded along his shoulders in a shower of goose bumps. "I have as much at stake in this ranch as you do, Charlie. I want to be here. I am your foreman and it is my job to take care of the stock."

"Fine. We'll stay out here together and keep each other company." She moved to the edge of the fencing and flipped on the radio to some country music. George Strait sang *I Cross My Heart* in the background. "I'm going to go make some coffee. It's going to be a long night."

He watched her walk down the long path to the double doors and out into the night. She was right. Long night wouldn't even cover it if he knew anything at all.

* * * *

Caleb glanced over the fencing several hours later to see Charlie curled up on a blanket on top of a bench along the stall siding. Her hand was beneath her cheek, her long lashes lay against her skin, and her breathing was slow and even. Her hair had partially fallen out of the ponytail she'd put it in, to caress her neck. She was the sexiest thing he'd ever seen even with dark circles under her eyes.

He learned over the last several days how much the ranch meant to her. She'd put in long hours every day helping him do chores, feed the animals, fix fences, and even the nights he'd gone home, the light would still be on in her office.

They'd been taking turns walking the stallion around the arena every time he went to lay down. Exhaustion had claimed her a couple of hours ago when she'd stumbled as she walked the animal, almost falling flat on her face in the dirt. He'd insisted she go in the house and go to bed, but she'd balked and instead took to the bench, telling him to wake her in an hour. Unable to keep from worrying about her, he let her sleep while he continued to walk.

The sun would be coming up soon. In fact, he could see the sky beginning to lighten through the open door.

If he wasn't mistaken, Charlie had said the mares would be arriving later this afternoon, but he wasn't sure they were ready. Plus, they would have to keep the stallion secured until he was better. It would be a bad idea to let him around the mares right now. Charlie had also mentioned two client horses arriving this morning. The timing for the stallion to get colic couldn't have been worse. They could've used a few more days.

Caleb heard the clank of the gate on the arena as he rounded the far side. When he glanced over his shoulder, Charlie was walking toward him.

"Why didn't you wake me?"

"You were sleeping so soundly, I didn't want to bother you."

A frown marred her face, giving her the bossy look he remembered from a few days ago. "How's he doing?"

"He seems to be doing a little better. I am not a vet, but he did leave us a little present in the corner."

"Well, that's a good sign. I sure hope he bounces back from this quickly."

The smooth polyester of the lead rope against his palm kept his mind on the horse and not on the gorgeous woman who looked rumpled enough to have just crawled out of bed. "I've seen some horses turn around in a day or two where others have taken months."

Charlie smoothed her hair back, undid her ponytail, and retied it. "I know. Let's hope that the fact that he's pretty healthy will mean this won't take him down for long."

Caleb couldn't keep his eyes from tracing the swell of her breasts as they pushed against her shirt. Remembering how those felt in his palms, his fingers began to tingle with the need to lift that t-shirt over her head, and press her against the fence. Her legs would wrap around his waist, pressing her hot pussy against his aching cock.

The pop and crunch of gravel indicated a vehicle coming up the driveway, dragging his thoughts back to the present. Caleb walked the horse toward the fence, hoping it was Doc Millburn. He could really use to catch a few hours of sleep even though his dreams would be disturbed by thoughts of Charlie.

"I'll see who it is," Charlie said over her shoulder as she headed toward the door.

The murmur of voices could be heard a few moments later, right before Charlie and someone he didn't know appeared near the arena.

Charlie's hands were buried in her front pockets giving him the idea she wasn't comfortable with the new arrival. "Caleb Armstrong, this is Aaron Tripper. Aaron, this is Caleb."

Aaron stepped forward, his hand out in greeting. "Nice to meet you, Caleb. Charlie tells me you're her foreman."

"That's right."

"Do you have a lot of experience with cutting horses?"

"Been working with them most my life." Caleb didn't like the looks of this guy or the way he possessively had his arm around Charlie's shoulder.

"Aaron's one of my clients. He has brought his gelding for training."

"And knowing you, sweetie, he will be one of the best-trained horses on the circuit."

Charlie ducked out from under his arm and positioned herself closer to the wall. "You do know I may not be working with him personally. I have another trainer, as well as Caleb, who will be working with new prospects."

Aaron's eyes narrowed as he pushed his cowboy hat back on his forehead. "I trust your judgment, Charlie."

"Good. And I trust Caleb with every animal here." Silence surrounded them for a moment, the only sound was nickering in the distance. "Well, let's get your boy out of the trailer and get him settled."

The two of them disappeared toward the big bay doors. Caleb stared after them for a few moments before he began to walk the stallion again. He had work to do and didn't include getting all possessive over Charlie in front of her clients. He would save the discussion of her relationship with Aaron for later.

* * * *

Once Aaron's gelding was in his stall, Charlie ushered Aaron back to his truck to get him on his way.

"How about dinner and a drink tonight?" Aaron took a piece of her hair between his fingers and tucked it behind her ear.

The familiarity of the gesture bothered her, but she couldn't afford to alienate right now. "I'm sorry, but I just have too much to do. With the stallion being colicky, I've already been up all night and I really need to catch a nap. Unfortunately, my mares should be showing up today, so we'll need to get them settled as well."

"A nice meal, a drink or two, and good company would do you good." He ran his fingertips down her cheek.

Now I am uncomfortable. Not that she didn't like Aaron, but their past relationship had ended badly. Obviously, Aaron hadn't gotten over it as easily as she had thought. She didn't want to encourage him in any way, but her feelings for him were over long ago. "Aaron, really, I can't. Trying to run the ranch, getting new clients, and developing our breeding program have to be my priorities. I really don't have time for a personal life."

He crowded closer, almost pinning her against the side of his truck. "I miss you, Charlie. We were good together, babe. I think we could be again."

Her hands came up to push him back.

He grabbed her wrists in his iron grasp. "I want you and make no mistake, I will have you."

The determined look in his eyes frightened her. He'd never been physically abusive, although right now she wasn't so sure that might not be the case if he was given the chance.

A low warning growl forced him to take a step back. Charlie glanced down to see Sparky with his gaze fixed on Aaron. The dog growled again, baring his teeth as he positioned himself next to Charlie. Apparently, Sparky had taken a liking to her and was going to protect her. She rested her hand on the dog's head, slowly stroking the soft fur. "I think you need to leave, Aaron. Please don't return unless you call first. Your gelding should be ready in six to eight weeks. I will call you with updates once a week. This is strictly a business relationship, remember that."

Aaron's only response was to narrow his eyes for a moment before he climbed into his truck and turned over his engine.

Her stomach knotted until his taillights had disappeared.

Caleb's hand settled on her hip, making her jump. "Are you okay?"

She turned toward him, buried her face in his chest, and heaved a heavy sigh as tears shimmered on the surface. *I won't let Aaron get to me. He's in my past and I'm done with all of that.*

He wrapped his arms around her, pulling her close. "What happened?"

"It was nothing," she whispered.

"You're shaking, so it was more than nothing."

After a moment, she stepped back. "I really don't want to talk about it right now. How is the stallion?"

"He's in his stall. We'll need to watch him closely for several days just to make sure he's going to be okay."

The sun had fully risen, bathing the yard in a bright yellow glow, brightening her mood slightly. She wouldn't allow Aaron to get to her. "Would you like some coffee?"

"I could really use some."

"I'll go grab a couple of cups and meet you in the barn." She took a few steps toward the house, but stopped and looked back. "Thanks."

"For what?"

"For everything."

Their gazes met for a moment before she mentally shook herself and continued on to the house. Men could cause you to do crazy things. If she wasn't careful she would find herself head over heels and being stupid all over again. That was one thing she couldn't afford.

The moment she stepped into the kitchen, she let out a long slow breath. *What a fucking mess this turned out to be. I don't need to piss off Aaron since he's a client, but I sure don't need him to try anything.* Her time with him had been brief although he'd went right into the I love you's pretty quickly. He'd been her rebound after her marriage, a weekend in a new town when she'd been searching for the property she wanted to buy to start her ranch. Dallas interested her, or the outskirts anyway, as a place to check out.

They'd met at the real estate office she'd stopped to see what listings they might have had. He'd been sitting behind a desk and when he glanced up, his gaze had been cold at first but warmed pleasantly. Getting to his feet, he'd come forward with his hand out, enveloping hers in his grasp. A trip to a restaurant around the corner, a few cups of coffee later, and he'd had her promise to come back the next day so he could show her some properties.

Nothing had appealed to her when they looked. He'd tried, he really had. She had been very particular about what she wanted in the property she invested in for her training facility. A house was a must along with an arena, outbuildings, stalls, and pasture. The house didn't need to be perfect since she had plans to remodel it anyway, which is why this property in Shadow had been perfect. It gave her a reason to get out of Dallas.

Aaron had become possessive, trying to tell her what to do, where to go, what to wear, and who her friends could be. The minute she could, she bailed out of the relationship and he'd gone ballistic, breaking some of her things, and stalking her wherever she went.

Keeping her location a secret hadn't worked. He'd found her through the registers that list training facilities and trainers. Her name was plastered all over the horse training community. It hadn't taken him long to figure out how to get to her through wanting to have her train a horse for him. He wasn't a rider, not even a horse person really. He planned to invest in the horse, have someone else ride him in competition, and when he won, he'd sell the stud rights.

She braced her hands on the sink and glanced out the window. Caleb moved around the barn, in and out the big doors as he started chores. Watching him was a pleasure she could indulge in for now. His movements were magnificent, all muscle, grace, sexiness. How they'd ended up becoming lovers, she wasn't sure. Somehow it felt right. Unfortunately, it wasn't something she could spoil herself with for the long term. Things would certainly come to an end eventually.

Her stomach clenched at the thought. Stopping this rollercoaster of a ride didn't appeal at all.

Later.

For now, she would enjoy the ride and relish the way her blood sizzled whenever he touched her. *His hands on me feel like being too close to an open flame. My body isn't my own. It belongs to him.*

Temporarily. *This is only temporary. I have to keep telling myself that.*

Chapter Eleven

Amy stepped out of her truck, shut the door, and headed toward the barn to meet him in the doorway. "Caleb."

"Amy. How are you?"

"Good. I'm ready to start work."

"Great. We have two for you to work with for now. A friend of Charlie's brought his gelding in this morning. He's in stall three."

"I heard in town you had a colicky stallion."

"We do. Charlie and I have been up all night keeping him walking."

"Shit. I'm sorry. If you would have called, I would have come out and taken a turn so you two could have gotten some sleep."

"I didn't think about it. Doc Millburn came out and checked him over. He said the stallion should be okay, but we needed to watch him. He should be out this morning to do a once over."

She tilted her head to the side, giving him a lingering look. "You look like shit, Caleb."

"Thanks."

"Just being truthful."

Charlie came out of the house carrying two travel mugs of what he hoped was strong coffee. "Hey, Amy."

"Mornin'."

"Did Caleb fill you in?"

"Yes, ma'am. I'll get your gelding moving this morning and then we can evaluate the new boy this afternoon if that works for you?"

"Sure does. I want to see how you do with Champ in the arena. I have a cow track set up on the far end. I have worked with him a little, but not much so you should probably run through the basics and see how he handles that before you get going too far."

"Sounds good." Amy moved into the darkness of the barn, heading down the center aisle. "Tack room down here?"

"Yes."

"Great. Any particular bridle or saddle I need to use?"

"Nope." Man, he was tired and downright cranky. He didn't need to be that way with Amy, he guessed. It wasn't like there was anything there anymore or ever was, but this first day on the new job for her could be uncomfortable. Too bad he hadn't had any sleep since night before last and even then, it had been riddled with dreams of Charlie even after they'd made love.

Sex in the shower had been off the charts. Hell, sex with her in any position or on any surface was phenomenal, but he needed to figure out where they were going with all of this. He frowned as his thoughts ricocheted around in his brain, not settling on anything worth a damn.

"You okay?" she asked, touching his bare arm.

"Yeah, just tired." He settled his hat back on his head, trying to ease the pounding behind his eyes.

"Amy is here. I can guide her in what needs to be done. Why don't you go get a few hours of sleep?"

"I've got too much to do today to sleep."

Doc Millburn's truck rattled down the driveway toward them, spewing dust in the air that followed him.

Caleb stepped forward as he slid to a stop in the gravel. "Doc."

"Hey, Caleb. How's the stallion this morning?"

"Doing better, I think. We've been watching him and walking him all night."

Doc slammed the truck door. "Well, let's go see."

When they approached the stall, the stallion stuck his head out over the half-door as the vet scratched him behind the ears. "You're looking better, big fella." He stepped inside the stall. "Let's take a listen."

After a thorough exam, Doc Millburn said, "His bowels sound improved. I think he'll pull through without too much difficulty, but keep a close eye on him for the next several days. Make sure he's going to the bathroom and let him eat a little at a time so we don't overload his system. Feed him a few times a day in smaller amounts. Watch his water, too."

"Got it," Charlie replied as she shut the stall door behind him when he came out. "Thank you, Dr. Millburn. You don't know how much I appreciate this."

"That's my job, girl. I love animals and I love taking care of them. Been doing it for nigh on forty years and I don't aim to quit anytime soon." He tipped his battered cowboy hat and headed for his truck.

"Can I get you some lemonade or something before you go?"

"No thank you. I have a couple more stops to make before I meet some of the locals at the coffee shop in town." He slipped inside the cab and rolled the window down. "You take care and call me if there seems to be a problem."

"I will. Thank you again."

He smiled and waved as be backed out and headed for the highway.

Caleb released a heavy sigh and raked his hands through his hair before setting his hat back on his head. Weariness dragged him down like the rush of river water over your head. His neck had knots on top of knots and his legs were dragging as if they had lead weights attached to the ankles. He hadn't stayed up all night walking a horse in a long time. A glance at Charlie revealed the tiredness in her eyes. The lines around her mouth were deeper this morning and the dark circles seemed more prominent. "We might as well get started with chores while Amy is working the gelding."

Charlie leaned against the side of the barn. "Yeah. I need to make sure the stalls are ready for the mares arriving today."

"What time?"

"Not sure." She sighed heavily and pushed off the wall. "Better get started."

Unable to help himself, he leaned in and kissed her on the mouth, savoring the taste of coffee and chocolate before lifting his head.

Her lips lifted in a soft smile as she touched his chest for a moment. "Thank you. I needed that."

"Me too." He draped an arm over her shoulders, guiding her inside the barn. A square shovel sat tucked in the corner of the tool room, next to the wheelbarrow. He took it by the handle, laid it inside and headed down the walkway toward the back of the barn. The stalls were mostly clean, they just needed a new layer of sawdust on the floor, fresh water, and checked over for anything that might injure the mares.

"I'm going to go check on Amy and see how she's doing."

"Sounds like a good plan." He glanced at his watch. Damn, it was only nine am. They had a long day ahead of them without much of a break in sight.

He watched Charlie walk toward the arena, her cute little ass swaying back and forth in her jeans. The heart shape made his palms itch to grab it and hold on tight as he fucked her against the wall. Oh wait, they did that yesterday in the shower. A chuckle escaped his lips while he went back to gathering everything he needed. The hard-on he sported now would make shoveling interesting, but he didn't have much of a choice. Work had to be done with or without an erection.

His thoughts drifted while he worked. It didn't take much brain power to shovel shavings. Mentally making a list of the things he needed to do today would keep his mind busy, at least for a little while. He would have to catalog the mares when they came in this afternoon, but he also had to make files for the stallion and the geldings. Those would be important since they would have to keep track of their training very well in order to be paid for their efforts. Cutting horse training could be very lucrative for the trainers if everything was done accordingly.

After an hour or so, he took a break to watch the two women in the arena. Charlie stood off the side while she watched Amy run her horse through its paces.

The moment Amy finished her current run, she trotted him over to Charlie.

He couldn't hear what they talked about from where he leaned against the railing, but he saw Amy dismount and Charlie take the reins.

This would be interesting. He'd never seen Charlie do a cutting routine on a horse.

Charlie mounted the gelding and took him toward where the cow track was strung across the arena at the far end. With the remote in her hand, she started the pattern she'd programmed into the computer.

The gelding took off toward the flag, keeping himself just behind it and turning toward it the minute it headed the other direction. The gelding led with his shoulder a couple of times and Charlie corrected him quickly by turning him in a few circles and backing him up to take that sensation away. As she started the flag again, the gelding kept watching as the thing moved, only losing his concentration a few times. The animal still needed some work, but he was doing well.

Caleb could tell Charlie guided the animal with an expertise he hadn't seen in another trainer in a very long time. *Damn, she's good.*

When she'd taken the gelding through an entire series, she trotted him back to where Amy had stayed along the fence.

Since he'd finished what he was doing, he followed her over.

"So can you see where I went with him?" Charlie said, handing Amy the reins.

"Yes, ma'am. He already does so well, I'm not sure what more you want me to work with him on."

"He needs more on leading with his nose and then we can bring in a few cows for him to work with. A few months of that and he'll be ready to be sold or go on to competition. I think my dad is looking to use him in the next season."

"When are you bringing some cows in?" Caleb asked as he stopped next to her. "I will have to check on some of the fences before that happens so they don't go wandering down the road."

Charlie smiled when she looked up. "Not for a couple of weeks or so. I would like to have more than just Champ ready to work with the real cattle before I bring them in. He can do additional with the cow track in the meantime."

"Are any of the other horses this far along?" Amy asked.

"I don't know about Aaron's horse. I haven't seen him move yet and I didn't want to get into a discussion with Aaron about him." Charlie glanced at him before focusing back on Amy. "There is a rocky history between us."

"Why did you take on his animal then?"

Charlie shrugged. "I'm not sure except that we need the animals. He has connections in Dallas that we need to make this operation work. Pissing him off would not be a good idea."

"A little ass-kissing then."

"Yeah."

Amy mounted the gelding again. "Let me run him a few more times before I put him away and then I'll bring out the other gelding to see what he's capable of. Do you know if he's had any training at all?"

"I don't, but my guess is no. Aaron is only after the investment, not the animal itself."

"Oh. Gotcha."

Charlie turned toward him and tipped her head, indicating he should follow her toward the stalls. Unsure of what it was all about, he stepped up beside her until they were out of earshot of Amy.

"What's up?"

"Watch her with the horses. I caught her subtle spurring with her heels. I don't want the animals spurred. That makes for a jumpy horse and depending on how much it's done, borders on abuse in my book. I haven't met a horse yet that needed that."

"I agree. I'll keep an eye on her."

They eased on around the corner where Amy couldn't see them. Charlie reached up on tiptoes to brush her lips over his. The softness reminded him of the place on the inside of her thighs where he'd kissed her. He hummed his appreciation as she stepped back.

"We have to be careful. I don't want Amy knowing about us."

"Why not?"

"It's not good practice to be messing with the staff."

She thought of him only as staff? *Oh, fucking hell no.* That wasn't going to work for him. No siree. "One of the staff? That's all you think of me, Charlie?"

"Well, no, but I have to keep up appearances. There is a history between you and Amy and if she finds out we are sleeping together, she could cause problems with the locals. I don't need that, Caleb. You of all people should understand where I am coming from with this."

He stepped back away from her and moved several feet away with his back to her. His composure was shot at the moment. Weariness made him cranky and the last thing he wanted to do was to lose his temper.

Her hand came down on his shoulder and he stiffened beneath her touch. "Caleb?"

"Yeah, whatever, Charlie. If you don't want people to know we are lovers, then so be it. I'll do my best to stay out of your bed except when you say so. You are the boss." He turned toward her, tipped his hat and walked out of the barn. His ears heated from the rage washing through him. Humiliation burned low in his gut. Obviously, he wasn't good enough for her. To hell with that. She could find someone else to warm her bed. He wasn't about to become someone's fuck toy.

* * * *

Charlie stood with her mouth open as she watched Caleb walk out. *What the hell was that all about?*

She turned toward the sound of horses' hooves as Amy came up beside her.

"Ma'am?"

"Yes?"

"Can you show me where the grain is kept? I'll feed Champ before I get the other gelding out to work him."

"Sure. And you don't have to call me ma'am. Charlie is fine."

"Yes, ma'am."

Amy took Champ to the tie down area, clipped him to the tie posts, and stripped him of his tack.

Charlie stopped at the tack room door and showed her a larger hay and grain storage area next to it. "The grain is in here. You can give him a full bucket, check his water, and give him a couple of flakes of hay. That should do him for the day. We can turn him out a little later after he's cooled down."

"I'll use the same tack on the other gelding if that's okay."

"It should be fine. You might have to make some adjustments for his stature. He's a bit larger in the head and chest than Champ is."

"No problem."

Amy fiddled with the halter between her fingers for a moment.

"Something else bothering you, Amy?"

"Well, I wanted to ask you a question."

"What's that?"

"How well do you know Caleb? I know you are aware we went out a while back, but I wanted to make sure you understood my side of things. I'm sure he told you his."

"Yes, he did, but I really don't need…"

"Hear me out, okay?" Amy dropped her gaze to the floor as she sighed. "I'm not sure really where to begin."

"At the beginning?"

Amy chuckled. "Yeah, that would be all right, I guess. Caleb and I have known each other a long time. We went to school together here. He's been a crush for me since high school. I wanted to go out with him for so long, when it fell into my lap, I went a little crazy. We were both at the bar in town. I was with a group of my friends and he was hanging with some of his playing pool." She moved over to run her hand down Champ's nose. "He was a little drunk, I think, but when he came up to me, he asked me out for dinner and a movie. I couldn't believe Caleb Armstrong asked me out."

Charlie wasn't sure where this whole conversation was going. Did she really care why Caleb and Amy went out? No, but since they were both employees of hers now, she'd better know their background in case there was a problem down the road. Never mind the fact that she and Caleb were now lovers.

"Anyway, we went out for a couple of months. I thought things were moving along great. We'd become exclusive or at least I thought so, and then *bam* he dropped me like a hot rock. When I asked him what the problem was, the only response I got out of him was to say he'd had a good time with me and now he had to move onto someone else." Amy looked up and Charlie could see something in her gaze she wasn't sure about. "I guess I went a little crazy."

"What do you mean?" Charlie asked, knowing what Caleb had told her.

"I did some damage to his truck."

"Oh?"

Amy cringed as she continued, "Yeah. Quite a bit of damage actually." She took a couple of steps toward Charlie. "But things are fine now. It was a while ago and I've moved on, we both have, I think. I know Caleb has dated some since then, and I've found a nice guy that I think could turn into something really good."

"Are you okay working under Caleb here on the ranch?"

"Yes. I hope Caleb finds a nice girl to settle down with. He's been such a player for a long time that he has a really bad reputation here in town. He's a damned good guy, but he's hard on the women around here."

Charlie wasn't sure she liked the sound of that. Caleb was a player. After her marriage, she didn't need that type of guy in her life or did she? Relationships weren't something she was looking for, right?

"Anyway, I'd better get Champ unsaddled so I can get to work on that new fella." Amy came in for a hug. "Thanks for listening and I hope you aren't disappointed in my work."

"As long as the horses are taken care of and trained properly, we shouldn't have any issues at all."

"Right."

When Amy took Champ into his stall and got him settled, Charlie thought about what she'd said. Not sure where Caleb had taken off to, she walked out of the barn and stopped in her tracks.

Sparky ran back and forth along the fence line, his nose to the ground. A shrill bark echoed every few moments when he found something to chase. Stripped of his shirt, Caleb was bent on one knee hammering the hell out of a nail on some fencing several yards away. His back glistened with sweat, stretching and moving with each swing.

Her mouth went dry at the sight. All those muscles on display played hell with her libido. She wanted him. No doubt about it. He could take her any way he wanted, over the side of the bed, in the hayloft amongst the scattered straw, or on a blanket under the stars. She didn't care.

The way he'd disappeared earlier, she'd apparently committed some kind of dastardly sin, but she wasn't sure what. She went over the scene in her brain, every last syllable of the conversation, and still, she couldn't figure out what she'd done wrong. Something had sure pissed him off. Maybe she should leave him alone for a bit. A fight wasn't what she needed right now.

The noon day sun had begun to heat the area. She needed something to wet her throat and some lemonade sounded really good. A pitcher she'd made the other day still sat in the refrigerator. Caleb might like some as well. *No, I need to let him cool off. The lack of sleep wasn't helping either of them.*

The screen door banged shut behind her as she went inside and headed to the refrigerator. She had some work to do on the books today as they waited for the mares to arrive. Caleb was going to be working on fencing, apparently, and Amy was busy with the horses. Things needed to be left as they were, otherwise shit might hit the fan.

A loud explosion rocked the house on its foundation, shattering glass in the kitchen as shards rained down on her head where she landed on the floor. The world tilted sideways as she lifted her hand to touch her head. It came back coated in blood.

Chapter Twelve

Caleb shook his head, trying to stop the ringing in his ears as he focused on the ground beneath his hands. *What in the hell just happened?* Everything was muddled in his brain, making it hard to think for a moment. Had he lost consciousness? He wasn't sure. All he knew at this point was something had exploded, throwing him to the ground near where he'd been repairing a fence some several hundred yards from the barn. Sparky nudged his hand before circling around him several times.

The barn. *Shit. Where were Amy and Charlie?*

He climbed to his feet, staggering for a second. The barn looked to be in one piece. His attention turned to the house. The windows in the kitchen were gone, the corner of the house wasn't there anymore.

Holy fuck! "Charlie!" He began to run, his steps not even or coordinated very well but he had to get to the house to make sure she wasn't in there. She'd still been in the barn when he'd went outside.

"Charlie! Where are you?"

Amy stumbled out of the barn. "Caleb? What happened?"

"I don't know. Where is Charlie?"

"She left me in the barn a little bit ago. I don't know for sure where she went."

He ran for the house. *Please God, don't let her be hurt. I'll do anything you want, just let her be okay.*

The front door hung on the hinges at an awkward angle as he pushed through the doorway calling her name. "Charlie?"

He stopped in the hallway to listen for any sounds, unsure of where to look first.

A soft moan reached his ears over the pounding of his heart. He stopped breathing for a split second to try and locate the sound.

Kitchen.

He raced through the hallway and into the kitchen, his boots sliding on the broken glass.

The prone body on the floor moved slightly, another soft moan escaping her lips.

Moving slowly toward her, he knelt down near her head and whispered, "Charlie?"

Blood seeped from beneath her head on the tile floor, the puddle spreading out in a bright red stream.

Oh God. "Charlie, can you hear me?" He didn't want to move her as he debated on what to do next. *Call an ambulance.*

Charlie rolled over on her own, revealing a large gash on her forehead, but he knew something worse had to be underneath her if the blood was any indicator.

The moment he fished his cell phone out of his pocket, he dialed. "Nine one one. What's your emergency?"

"I need an ambulance right away. There has been an explosion on the old Chesler place. The new owner is bleeding a lot from the head."

"Are they breathing?"

"Yes."

"Hold pressure to the wound and we'll be right there."

"Thank you."

Caleb saw a towel lying on the countertop a few feet away. It would have to do until the ambulance got there.

He reached under her head trying to position the towel to staunch the flow of blood. He didn't care if his hand was cut up in the process from the glass. All he knew was he needed to stop the bleeding.

Charlie's eyes opened before she moaned again and slammed them shut. "Holy shit."

"You'll be okay. Ambulance is on the way."

"What happened?"

"I'm not sure. An explosion of some kind. It blew out your windows in here, and I'm assuming the flying glass hit you."

"I must have lost consciousness when I fell."

"Are you hurt anywhere else?"

She touched her fingers to her forehead, the tips coming back with a lot of blood. Her hands started to shake. "Oh God. Blood. I don't do blood."

"You'll be okay. Close your eyes and lie still. I'm right here."

"Are the horses all right?"

"Amy is out there with them. I'm sure they are fine."

"You didn't check on them?"

"No, Charlie, I was a little more worried about where you were and if you were okay."

"I'm fine if you want to go check on them."

"They weren't making any noise when I was looking for you. Amy was still with the gelding in the arena and the other two were in their stalls. I'll go out there as soon as the ambulance arrives to take over caring for you." He pushed a piece of hair off her forehead. The terror he'd felt when he wasn't sure where she was had lost the squeezing grip it held on his heart. Her injuries weren't life threatening so he could breathe again.

"Caleb?"

"Yeah?"

"Thank you for being here. I don't know what I would do without you."

"I have to take care of my girl, right?"

Her brows furrowed between her eyes as her nose wrinkled a little. "Your girl?"

"At least for now, you are my girl. I protect what is mine."

* * * *

The wail of ambulance sirens could be heard in the distance as she looked up into Caleb's eyes. *I protect what is mine.* She wasn't sure how to take that last line, but right now her head hurt too much to think. Sleeping sounded mighty nice at the moment.

"Charlie, you need to stay awake. I know you want to sleep, but I don't think that's a good idea right now. You have a head injury and until the paramedics look at you, you shouldn't sleep."

"I'm so tired."

"I know, baby. Tell me more about Champ. What kind of groundwork did you do with him before? I was very impressed when you took him to rein in the arena. You're damn good at what you do."

The compliment surprised her in a way. Caleb wasn't the type of man to give them lightly. "Thank you. He still needs some work, but I think we should be able to sell him in a few months for a good price. He performs well."

"Yes, he does. I'm excited to see him work a real cow. I think he'll do great."

Ambulance sirens stopped as they heard clomping of boots on the wooden stairs.

"In here guys!"

The paramedics brought in a gurney and their equipment. "What's going on, Caleb?"

He shouldn't have been surprised to recognize both men. After all, he'd grown up here. "Noah. Mason. I'm glad you are here. This is Charlie. She owns the place. We had some kind of explosion about fifteen minutes ago. I have no idea where or why, but it blew out the windows on the kitchen and Charlie lost consciousness when she hit the floor or before. I'm not sure. I wasn't in here. I found her like this. She has a wound to the back of her head that is bleeding a lot. I have been holding pressure on it."

Noah knelt down at Charlie's side as he opened his box. "What's your name, sweetheart?"

She frowned as she looked up at Caleb. "Charlie Abrams."

"Do you know where you are?"

"My house in Shadow. I bought it several months ago."

"Good. Do you know what the date is?"

She recited the date before she asked, "Why all the questions?"

"It gives me an idea of how hurt you are. You've done fine with them, so I am thinking the damage is minimal, but we'll let the doctor decide that at the hospital."

"Hospital?" She tried to sit up, but Caleb pushed her back down. "I'm not going to the hospital, Caleb. I don't need a doctor. I'm fine."

"You aren't fine, baby. You lost consciousness, which is serious. You probably have a deep gash on the back of your head since it is still bleeding. You need to see a doctor."

"I hate doctors. I hate hospitals. I'm not going."

"Yes you are if I have to haul your ass into the back of that ambulance myself."

Noah and Mason chuckled while Noah continued to check her over from the cut on her forehead to her toes and Mason put the blood pressure cuff on her arm. "Sit up for me for a second."

When she managed to get into an upright position, her head started to feel fuzzy and her vision narrowed.

"Easy, darlin'."

Noah looked at the back of her head and prodded a little with his fingers. "Shit, that hurts!"

"You have a very large laceration that will need stitches and I'm sure they'll need to make sure there aren't any shards of glass in there. You also have one on your forehead that might need stitches as well. For now, I'm going to bandage both and go from there." He moved in front of her and shined a very bright light into her eyes.

"My head is killing me."

"I'll give you something for pain once we get into the ambulance. It won't be anything too strong since we don't want you to sleep until they do a few tests on you in the emergency room." He got to his feet and pulled a radio from his belt. "Shadow ER this is truck four. Do you copy?"

"Shadow ER, go ahead truck four."

"How old are you, Charlie?"

"Twenty-eight."

"Shadow ER, I have a twenty-eight-year-old female who has a large laceration to the posterior cranium and also a laceration to her forehead. Vital signs are blood pressure one-twenty-eight over sixty-five, heart rate eighty, and respirations are eighteen. She is alert and oriented although is complaining of lightheadedness. She did lose consciousness prior to our arrival. Unknown how long. There is a possibility of glass in the wounds as there is a lot of shattered glass at the scene. There was an apparent explosion on site of unknown origin."

"Ten four, truck four. What is your ETA?"

"Ten minutes."

"Copy. See you then."

They helped her to sit on the gurney, swung her around so she was lying down, and then strapped her in like a sack of potatoes. Her whole body began to shake as the realization of the situation sank in.

Noah grabbed a blanket and tucked her in.

"Thanks."

"You're welcome."

As they wheeled her out to the ambulance Amy came out of the barn. "What's going on?"

"Charlie was hurt. They are taking her to the hospital to be checked out."

"How are the horses?" Charlie asked before they could slide her inside.

"They are fine. A little spooked, but they'll be okay."

"Thanks, Amy."

"No problem. I'll stay until Caleb or you are back."

"I appreciate it."

Caleb moved next to Amy as they pushed Charlie into the ambulance. She couldn't hear what he said, but she was sure he would take care of things. That's just the way he was.

About ten minutes later, they pulled into the ambulance bay at the hospital. It was her first view of the place and her impression hadn't been decided.

They wheeled her into a room to the left before lifting her to the more stable bed.

Her head continued to pound with the beat of her heart, leaving her thoughts unclear. "Where is Caleb?"

"I'm sorry, Ms. Abrams, but I don't know who Caleb is."

"He's my foreman. He lives on the ranch with me. He should be here. I need him here."

"I'll see if he is out in the waiting room, but for right now, you need to calm down and let me take a look at you so the doctor can come in and treat you."

"What's your name?"

"Debbie."

"Call me Charlie." The nurse's gaze caught hers with a confused look. "My name is Charlene, but everyone calls me Charlie."

"All right then. Charlie it is." Debbie took her vital signs, checked her pupils, and cut off her clothes.

"Hey!"

"I'm sorry, but I have to make sure there aren't any other injuries."

"You didn't have to cut them. I would have taken them off."

"You don't need to be moving with your injuries and at this point, I don't know if there are any others."

Charlie glared at Debbie as she continued with the scissors until she had every stitch of her clothes off. *Damn. I'll have to go shopping now. She cut my best bra!*

Once the exam was over, Debbie helped her into a backless piece of clothing that did nothing to hide any of her body parts but was better than naked, not by much though.

"Dr. King will be in shortly. We aren't too busy today so there shouldn't be any delay."

"Thanks." Charlie licked her dry lips. "Can I have some water, please?"

"Not yet. I need to see what tests Dr. King will want. Some you need to be NPO for, which means nothing by mouth."

"Great," she grumbled. "Just great."

Debbie laughed as she spread a blanket over her. "How about if I see if your friend is in the waiting room?"

"That would be awesome."

A few moments later, she felt a touch on her hand. When she opened her eyes, Caleb was standing next to the gurney. She didn't realize she'd closed her eyes.

"Hey."

"Hi." He threaded his fingers through hers, putting their hands palm to palm. "How do you feel?"

"Fine. I hope this is over soon."

"I'm sure it will be. Has the doctor been in?"

"Not yet."

"Ms. Abrams?"

"Yes?"

A very nice looking, blond man came in the room. He had very pretty green eyes, with a lock of hair hanging over the left eyebrow. "I'm Dr. King." After he moved around the other side of the bed, he lifted the bandage on her forehead and looked at the cut. "This one I can glue, I think. Sit up and let me see the one on the back."

Caleb helped her sit straight up, but the movement tore a moan from her lips.

The moment Dr. King touched the one on the back of her head, she winced and cried out.

"This one is more of an issue. It's very deep and I believe there may still be some glass in there. I will be sending you to CT for a scan and then we'll go from there." He ran his hands over her arms and legs. "Hurting anywhere else?"

"No."

"Did you lose consciousness?"

"Yes," Caleb answered for her. "When I found her, she was out."

"Do we know how long?"

"Not really. It was several minutes from the time the explosion happened to when I found her but I don't know if she was out the whole time."

Dr. King went through a series of questions on her name, the date, who the president was, and a couple others. She remembered everything, but those first few moments before the explosion. The image of Caleb's naked back in the sun as he fixed the fence was very clear. Her face heated at the thought.

"All right then. I'm going to have the nurse give you something for pain. The technician should be in shortly to get you for the tests in the radiology department. Once I have those results, we will see what else needs to be done. The back of your head will need to be stitched. I need to make sure there isn't any glass in the wound before I do that."

"Thank you."

"You're welcome. I'll be back as soon as I have everything."

The physician walked out the door, his broad shoulders stretching the material of his blue scrubs. He was very good looking and kind to boot. A woman could get used to looking into those expressive green eyes.

When she glanced back at Caleb, he had a frown on his face. "What?"

"Nothing."

"You look pissed."

"No, worried, yes."

"Any ideas on what would have caused an explosion like that? You were outside when it happened, right?"

"Yeah, I was, but I have no idea where or what exploded. Amy was in the barn with the gelding. I was knocked to the ground by the blast myself. The general direction was to the east."

"East. Huh. I don't even know who owns that property or anything. Do you?"

"No. An elderly couple owned it several years ago. I was under the impression it had been abandon when they went into a nursing home. Their kids didn't want it. They never sold it, I don't think."

Her head hurt beyond anything she could ever imagine, but thoughts kept ricocheting through her mind and she couldn't quiet them. Not understanding what might cause that type of explosion left her wondering. If the place was empty next door, surely it wasn't from anything over there. What might be on her property that would make this happen?

Debbie came in a few moments later. Her gaze went straight to Caleb before settling back on Charlie as she said, "I brought you something for pain."

Charlie wasn't sure what to make of the look. Debbie looked almost angry when she'd glanced his way. After this was all over, she'd have to ask him.

Two pills were given to her to swallow. "What is this?"

"Hydrocodone with Tylenol in it. It should ease the pain in your head."

A young man knocked on the door as she swallowed the medication. "I'm Tyler from radiology. I'm here to take you for your tests."

Charlie nodded as Caleb stepped back. "You'll be here when I get back, right?"

"I'm not going anywhere, darlin'. I'll be right here."

She smiled as Tyler wheeled her out the door, her gaze never leaving Caleb until he was out of sight. The thought of not having him close by made her sick to her stomach.

Lights rolled by overhead as the technician took her down the long hallway. She'd never had any tests done like this before, so she wasn't sure what to expect. The paramedics had put a needle in her arm in the ambulance, and now the thing was bugging her as she bent her arm. "Can we take this thing out?"

"No, ma'am. That needs to stay there. We aren't sure what other things we might need to do that we could use it for. We will be doing an x-ray for now."

"For what?"

"I'm not sure what the doctor is looking for. He wants one of your head and your neck."

"Okay, I guess."

"Can you stand?"

"I'm lightheaded when I stand up."

"I'll help you."

She moved to a sitting position on the gurney, moaning as her head started to swim and nausea rolled through her stomach. "I think I'm going to be sick."

"Breathe through your nose. Long deep breaths," Tyler said, holding her hand until the nausea eased.

"Okay. I think I'm good now."

"All right. I need you to stand over here by this metal piece on the wall. You'll have to hold really still. Do you think you can do that?"

"I'm not sure."

"Give it a try. If not, we can do something else."

She swayed slightly as she closed her eyes, willing her body to not betray her by being weak. It would only take a moment to get the pictures. She could do this.

The next thing she knew, Tyler was helping her back onto the gurney.

"You did great. The doctor should be able to do what needs done with these."

"Thanks for your help."

"My pleasure, ma'am."

The moment she made it back to her little cubicle, she looked for Caleb. *Where is he? He said he would be right here.* "Do you know where my friend is," she asked the nurse as soon as the gurney stopped by the wall.

"I'm sorry, but he said to tell you he had to leave."

"Did he say why?"

"No, other than he couldn't stay here any longer. He needed to do something very important and he could see you when you made it home. He made arrangements for you to take a cab home."

A cab? What the hell? Whatever needed him so badly obviously took precedence over her? *That tells me I mean very little to him.*

"Thank you for your help."

The pity she saw in the nurse's gaze rolled over her like a wave. If there was one thing she wouldn't tolerate from anyone was being brushed aside and pity? That emotion was for the weak and gullible, something she was not.

Chapter Thirteen

Caleb's slid his truck to a skidding stop in front of Charlie's house, before jumping out and rushing toward the barn.

Lights and sirens blared loudly from the fire truck, ambulance, and police car that were parked in front. Several hoses were strung from the truck toward the flames licking at the sky from the large structure. Sparky barked near the back of the fire truck at the spotted dog perched on top.

"The horses. Did they get the horses out?" he asked the first person he came to.

"I don't know, Caleb. Check over there." Daniel Miller was the local sheriff and an old friend of his. "I didn't see them bring any out."

Caleb turned to his left and rushed around the side of the burning building, praying with everything he had that the stallion and the two geldings had made it out. At first, he didn't see anything or anyone. Stupid as it seemed, he tried to go inside only to be beaten back by the flames. Nothing could be saved from what he could tell.

His steps took him a little further around the back until he saw Amy standing in the center of the paddock holding the reins of the stallion, another horse lying at her feet on its side. "Amy?"

"Oh, thank God you're here, Caleb. I don't know what happened. It was another explosion and then the next thing I knew, the barn was on fire."

He ran his hands down the side of the stallion. "He seems okay, just shaken up." When he glanced down, his stomach turned over. Aaron's gelding was the animal on the ground and he wasn't breathing. "What happened to him?"

Tears streamed down her face unchecked, streaking her cheeks with soot from the fire. "I couldn't get them all. I tried, Caleb, really I did. He was trapped in his stall. He broke down the door and ran out here, but he didn't make it very far before he dropped and stopped breathing."

"It's okay. You tried." *Shit. Aaron's going to have a cow when he finds out his gelding is dead.* "Where is Charlie's gelding?"

"I had him in the arena at the time, so he's safe." She shivered in the heat as she wrapped her arms around herself. "Where's Charlie?"

"She's at the hospital still getting checked out. I left as soon as I heard about the other explosion from one of the cops at the hospital. I figured she was in good hands. I set up for a cab to bring her home in case I don't get back there. I needed to see what kind of damage there was here."

Smoke curled toward the blue above as the flames began to die down. The fire department kept water streaming onto the structure in an attempt to stop anything else from catching fire.

The barn was a total loss from what he could tell.

He looked down at the dead horse. Thank God it wasn't the stallion. Charlie had sunk a huge amount into him for breeding purposes, although her insurance would have to pay Aaron for his horse. *I hope her premiums are paid up.* Burial would be a priority due to the heat. It wouldn't be long before the animal started to bloat up.

His thoughts turned to the explosions themselves as he gazed off toward where the hills rose gently above the horizon. What the hell was causing them? Charlie never said anything about gas out here. She didn't have propane on the house, so it couldn't be that. *These damn things are coming out of nowhere.*

As soon as Charlie got back from the hospital and things settled down here, he was going to do some investigating. Something wasn't right and he intended to find out what it was for everyone's sake. He headed toward where the backhoe tractor was stored and began digging a hole to put the dead animal in. It wouldn't take long. The ground was soft from the recent rain.

The moment he finished burying the horse, his cell phone rang in his pocket. When he pulled it out, he cringed. *Charlie.* "Hello?"

"Caleb? What happened? Where are you? You said you'd be in the room when I got back from the tests and now you are nowhere to be found. I thought you cared about me, even just a little, but I guess I was wrong." He heard her sniff.

"Charlie. I'm sorry, I had to come back to the ranch. There—"

"I don't care. You let me down again. I'm done. Apparently, I am nothing to you but a roll in sheets and I won't be that for anyone again. Pack your stuff and get off my land."

"Charlie, wait—"

"No, Caleb. I'm done."

The phone clicked in his ear. "What the hell? She hung up on me." He tried calling her back but the phone went straight to voicemail. She'd apparently shut the phone off. "God damn it to hell!"

"What's wrong?"

Realizing Amy stood nearby, his gaze went to her face for a moment as he let the phone call sink in. "I was just fired."

"Seriously? Charlie fired you. Why?"

"It's personal, but yeah, I guess I'm without a job." He turned and headed for his truck. What personal belongings he'd had on the ranch went up with the barn since his stuff was inside the tack room at the back.

"Caleb, wait. What's going on? What am I supposed to do with the stallion and the gelding?"

"Put them in the paddock for now until Charlie gets back, then ask her. I don't work here anymore."

He climbed into his truck, slammed the door and sat there for a moment watching the smoke curl up from the ashes of what was left. Charlie didn't think he cared. Problem was, he cared too much. He'd do what she asked, but this wasn't over yet. After a few days, he'd come back and try to talk some sense into her head. Crazy female. Didn't she know he was falling in love with her?

* * * *

Her hands shook as she set the phone down on the bed beside her. A lone tear slid down her cheek. Her gaze fixed on the white tiled ceiling above her. *He didn't care enough to stay at my bedside even when he said he'd be here when I got back.*

With her shattered heart, she took a deep breath and looked at the nurse. "When can I get out of here?"

"As soon as the doctor checks your tests and stitches up the back of your head. You have a very nasty laceration back there."

"Fine. Let's get this done so I can get out of here." Anger consumed her when she thought about Caleb leaving. Didn't he know she needed him here? Didn't he care at all?

Apparently not.

The doctor came in a few moments later with a small tray inside a plastic bag. "I need to stitch up the back of your head, Ms. Abrams. I will numb it up with some medication, but I will have to shave a little of your hair away so I can get to it properly."

"It's fine. Do what you need to do. I can wear it in a ponytail if I need to."

"Please sit forward and turn toward the nurse to your right and we will get this done."

He snipped away some hair, leaving a few strands on the bed beside her. She picked a piece up and ran it between her fingers thinking about when Caleb had done the same thing a few days ago after they'd made love.

After the initial sting of the medication, she didn't feel anything but a little pressure as the doctor stitched up her head.

"I won't put a bandage on it because it won't stay on anyway. Just keep it clean and dry if you can. You can wash your hair, but don't use any hair products for now. You will need to follow up with your doctor in a few days."

"I don't have one here. I haven't lived here long enough."

The doctor came around to the end of the gurney, threw away his bloody gloves, and then turned to face her. His eyes held concern even as the edges of his lips twitched in a small smile. "When you check out with the receptionist, they can give you the names of a few family practice physicians in the area. Pick one. They are all good people and take wonderful care of their patients."

"Thank you."

"You're welcome. I hope I don't see you in here again for a long time to come."

The nurse handed her some scrubs to wear home since they'd cut her clothing. "You can bring them back when you get settled at home."

"Thanks." After she changed, she took the paperwork the nurse handed her and slowly walked down the hallway toward the exit. Good thing she still carried her insurance, otherwise she would be paying through the nose for this visit to the emergency room. Between the ambulance ride and the tests alone would be thousands.

Once she finished with the receptionist and she had the names of the local physicians in her hands, she made her way outside. A cab sat near the entrance.

"Are you Charlie Abrams?"

"Yes."

"I was sent to take you home."

"You were?"

"Yes, ma'am." The driver opened the door on her side and held it while she climbed into the car. After he'd shut the door, he went back around to the driver's side, slid inside and started the vehicle. "You live on the old Chesler place?"

"That's the one."

"You got it." He pulled out of the driveway out onto the highway. "Heard there was some kind of explosion out there."

"Yes. That's why I was here. It blew out the windows of my house, threw me across the floor, knocked me unconscious and left me with a big gash in the back of my head."

"When was that?"

"A couple of hours ago, I guess. Why?"

"The fire trucks were just out there about thirty minutes ago. Heard the barn had gone up."

"What?" She leaned forward. "The barn? When was this?"

"It was on the scanner, oh, about maybe half an hour ago. Chatter at the diner said it was a total loss."

The blood drained from her face, leaving her head pounding harder than it had when she hit her head. *The barn. Oh my God! The horses!* "Hurry, please. I have to see the damage to my place. I didn't know anything about the barn."

"I'm real sorry, miss. I didn't know."

"It's okay. Just hurry."

The car sped down the road, fencing went flying by her window as she focused on the black smoke curling toward the sky in the distance. *Please God, let the animals be okay. Let Caleb be okay. Let Amy be okay.*

As they raced down the driveway toward her house, the shell of the barn came into focus.

"Oh my God," she whispered, unable to believe what she was seeing.

The car no more than stopped before she was pushing open the door and almost stumbling out. Amy turned toward her the minute she was out.

"Charlie, I am so sorry. I tried to stop the spread, but there was nothing I could do. Everything went up so fast."

Charlie grabbed her by the shoulders. "Where are the horses?"

"The stallion and your gelding are in the paddock. The other gelding didn't make it. He was in there too long and dropped as soon as he got outside."

"Aaron's gelding is dead?"

"Yes."

"Amy, where—where is Caleb?"

"He left right after you talked to him on the phone. Did you really fire him, Charlie? He rushed back here as soon as he heard about the fire in the barn. He told me to put the animals in the paddock. He even tried going back inside to save some of the tack but the flames were too bad."

"Caleb was here?"

"Yeah. What was with the phone call? You fired him. Why?"

"It's personal, Amy."

"Personal my ass."

Charlie felt heat rise up her face. This thing between her and Caleb wasn't any of Amy's business, but here she was letting her employee read her the riot act.

"I don't know what all is going on between you two, but from the way I see it, you've got something special. He never looked at me or any other woman in this town the way he looks at you. Caleb is a special guy. If you let him get away, you are a fool, Charlie. He's good for you and you're good for him. He's happy now, happier than I've ever seen him. He smiles a lot more than he ever used to and from what I've seen, you two could set fire to dry grass. I know you've been sleeping together. It's obvious by the way you two are around each other, the intimate smiles, the little touches when you think no one is paying attention. He is the best thing to happen to you and if you let him go, you will regret it for the rest of your life."

Charlie stood staring at Amy for several minutes before she turned on her heels and slowly walked toward the house. Too many thoughts were running through her head to focus on any one thing.

The moment she stepped inside, the glass crunched under her feet. The cheap flip flops the hospital gave her to wear home along with the scrubs, barely covered her feet, much less protected them from the glass. The closet next to the front door held her broom and dustpan. With the broom in her hands, she absently swept up the glass from the hall and worked her way into the kitchen.

Blood splattered the floor near the center of the room.

Must have been where I was laying.

She gingerly touched the back of her head, wincing as pain streaked through her skull. The independent her said she was better off without him, but the woman in her realized he held her together when she would have fallen apart. Strong women still needed someone sometimes, and right now she needed Caleb more than her next breath. Would he forgive her for being such a baby about everything when all he tried to do was save her ranch? She wouldn't know unless she tried.

Cell phone service sucked in these parts. Good thing she had a landline.

A yellow plastic phone hung on the wall in her kitchen, with its twist cord that could reach anywhere in the room if she stretched in. Most people probably wouldn't know how to use a rotary dial phone. Lucky for her grandma had one in her house.

She picked up the receiver and dialed Caleb's cell phone by memory, unsure if he would even answer her call.

"Caleb Armstrong," he said when he answered.

"Caleb, it's Charlie."

"Are you okay? There hasn't been another explosion, has there? Are you home?"

"Yes, I'm fine. No, nothing else has exploded. Yes, I'm home." She paused for a moment, debating on what to say. "I'm sorry, Caleb. I didn't mean what I said earlier when I was at the hospital. I didn't know you'd come back to the ranch because the barn was on fire and the horses were in jeopardy. I was being very juvenile about you leaving. I should have asked what was going on rather than jumping to conclusions about why you left. I was feeling very needy at the time, is all I can think of, and I took it out on you."

Silence stretched for what seemed like hours before she heard a sigh on the other end of the line.

"Stay there. I'll be there in a few minutes. I'm not far away."

The line clicked in her ear. *What does that mean?* She held the phone receiver away from her ear, staring at it for a few moments before hanging it back on the hook.

What would happen when he got there, she wasn't sure? At least he didn't sound mad.

Time clicked by at the speed of a snail. She could hear the ticking, reminding her of each second.

While she'd waited, she got the glass cleaned up so at least no one would cut their foot should they walk through without shoes on. His truck pulled into the drive in a spray of gravel as she leaned the broom against the wall and emptied the dustpan into the trash.

The door flew open, banging against the wall behind it.

"Charlie?"

"In the kitchen."

He rushed through the doorway, leaving no time for her to take a breath before he swept her up in his arms and his mouth came down hard on hers.

He consumed her, sliding his mouth over hers in a bruising kiss meant to communicate his passion and need.

When he finally lifted his head, he framed her face and pressed his forehead against hers. His breath hit her face is a warm caress as he tried to get his breathing under control. "How's your head?"

"Fine. They put in stitches back there, so I have a bald spot, but it's okay," she whispered.

The next moment her body was crushed to his chest as his arms wrapped around her. "God, I was so scared when I found you on the floor." His hands shook while he ran them down her back. "I had no idea what to do and that terrifies me. Seeing you hurt like that made me realize some things about us that I really need to think through. You've become a very important person in my life for no other reason than I can't see myself waking up in the morning without you beside me."

Was he saying he loved her? The connection between them had been growing since they met and her own feelings toward Caleb were becoming more than what she could fathom. Did she love him? Did she want him in her life from now on?

He moved back so he could look into her face as he traced her cheekbones with his thumbs. "You may not want to hear this, Charlie, because I know you've been hurt in the past and you are the type of woman who doesn't need a man in her life unless it's on her terms. You and I butt heads, that's a given, but what I am beginning to feel for you has no boundaries and no end. Is it love? Hell if I know, since I've never been in love before. All I can see is what's in front of me and that's you." He brushed his lips gently over hers. "I need you in my life."

Her heart hammered in her chest, taking her breath with it as she stared up into his eyes. Those same beautiful eyes who held so much in them now, she wasn't sure where to start. Did she love him? Maybe. It was definitely more than anything she'd felt before and something way beyond what she'd had with her ex. His right hand tucked a piece of hair behind her ear before returning to her face. She loved his touch on her skin. The calluses of a hardworking man felt like road bumps of life.

As he leaned in for another kiss, the earth moved beneath her feet. She looked up into his face and realized he could feel it too. "I've never had the earth move under me when a man kissed me."

"I would love to take credit for it, darlin', but it's not me. The earth really is moving."

"Earthquake? I didn't think we had those in Texas."

"Not normally." He kissed her nose. "We'll get back to this, but I think we need to find out what the hell is causing all of this on your property."

"I agree."

He took her hand and led her out to the paddock where the animals were now being housed. "Did they deliver the mares?"

"No. I hope you don't mind, but I had them redirected to Doc Millburn's place for now. He has plenty of room and they'll get good care until we can figure out where to put them."

She brought him to a stop with a tug on his hand. When he turned toward her, she touched the scruff on his cheek with her fingertips. The sensation was heady. "Thank you. I don't know what I would have done were you not here to take care of things."

"It's my job."

"I know, but you don't do it because it's your job. You do it because you care about this place as much as I do."

A tender smile lifted the corners of his mouth. "I do it because you are important to me." He kissed her lightly on the mouth. "Let's grab the ATV's and do some exploring. Something is going on here that we aren't privy to and we need to find out what."

They pulled out of the storage area a short time later, headed for the hills in the distance. She'd done some research on the ranches adjacent to her property and knew both were owned by ranching families, but there was a third piece of property on the south end. It connected along her fence line not far from her outbuildings and house. She hadn't been able to locate the name of the owner on that piece as it had been sold recently to some development company.

When they crested the hill overlooking that south property, she was stunned to see huge areas of development. Several sites had large machinery running at an incredible rate. They were tall steel structures, but she couldn't put her finger on what they were.

They got off the ATV's and snuck up the rocky incline to get a closer look.

"What are those?"

"If I'm not mistaken, they are structures for fracking."

"What the hell is fracking?"

"It's a slang term for hydraulic fracking which is used to force gas and oil from rock that isn't so forgiving as the old style of oil drilling."

"Those structures are way too close to my property line."

"Yes, they are." Caleb glanced at her before looking back over what they'd found. "Any idea who owns that property?"

"No. I tried finding out before I moved here, but some development company had bought it recently. I had hoped they were going to make it into a housing development, but it appears that wasn't their plan."

"No, I would say not." The rapid beat of his fingers on the rock under his hand made her aware of his agitation at the situation. "From what I understand about fracking, and admittedly it is very limited, they push large amounts of water into the ground to force the gas and oil to the surface. It's not illegal, but if for some reason this method of retrieving minerals is damaging your property, then they would have to cease procedures or reimburse you for damages."

"What kind of damages to my place?"

"There are chemicals released during the process that can hurt your animals, contaminate your water supplies, and yes, even cause explosions on your property."

"You aren't serious."

"Deadly serious."

They could see men moving around the structures, checking gauges, and measuring things as the steel piece of equipment continue to move in a slow, steady rhythm. *Clang, clang, clang.*

"We don't need to get caught snooping, but I think it is very important for us to find out who is behind the purchase of that property and make sure the EPA is aware of their practices. There are too many things that cause issues with fracking." Caleb backed down off the rocks with her on his heels until they reached the ATV's. "Let's head back to the house. We need to do some research."

Several minutes later, they drove through the back gate behind the paddock leading around the side of the covered arena. The second she rounded the corner, her heart stopped.

Chapter Fourteen

"Shit," she said as she brought her leg over and stepped onto the ground. Caleb was beside her in two steps.

"Easy, darlin'."

Sparky growled from his spot at Caleb's side. "Easy boy."

She glanced up into his face, taking strength from his hand on her hip. This was not going to be a pleasant meeting.

"Charlie. Where is my horse?"

"Well, Aaron, we need to talk. Can we go inside the house? It's very warm out here," she suggested taking a few steps toward the porch.

Aaron grabbed her arm and spun her around. Caleb growled low in his throat as he gripped Aaron's wrist and twisted.

"You will not put another hand on the lady."

"Lady? Fuck man. She's gotten to you, hasn't she?" He yanked on the man's arm until he forcibly stepped back. "Been fucking her, I bet."

Caleb pulled back his hand to punch the asshole in the face, but Charlie stopped his forward momentum in time to keep him from hitting Aaron.

"I'll handle this." She touched his cheek with her hand. "I can take care of him." She turned back toward Aaron. "Your gelding expired from smoke inhalation when the barn burned down this morning. Caleb buried him in the pasture near the back corner."

"You can't be serious! You killed my horse?"

"No, I did not. The barn caught fire. We were unable to get him out in time and he collapsed the moment he was out. He quit breathing, Aaron. There was nothing we could have done even if the vet had been right here. You know that."

"Do you have any idea how much that gelding was worth? His potential alone?"

"No, I'm afraid I don't. I will give you the information on my insurance carrier so you can contact them."

"Insurance won't be enough to cover him, so you'd better plan on something else. My attorney will be in touch." He turned on his heels and headed back to his vehicle. "And by the way, you might want to put this place up for sale because baby, you're going to lose everything you own." The door slammed shut behind him and he sprayed gravel as he gunned the truck down the driveway.

"I was afraid of this."

"You do have a good policy, right?"

She leaned her head on his chest as he wrapped his arms around her back. "Yes, but if he tries to get money for income potential, breeding rights now gone, and all that, he could ruin me before we've even begun."

The circle of his arms brought one word to her mind. *Home.* She sank further into his embrace, taking solace from his nearness

Aaron could ruin her. He would just to be spiteful. She would have to think of something to save her ranch.

Caleb held her for what seemed like hours as she stood absorbing everything she could. When she finally lifted her head, she sighed heavily and tried to shake off the feeling of impending doom she had deep in her chest. "We need to figure out where to stable the horses until we can rebuild the barn."

"I'll take care of it."

"The old barn will have to do, I guess. It's pretty run down though. We'll have to get some repairs done fast to make it doable."

"I'll get right on the repairs. The stallion and the gelding will be okay in the paddock for now." He snapped his fingers as a grin spread across his lips. "I'll call some friends. We'll have an old-fashioned barn raisin'. If you supply the food and beer, they'll come."

"You think so?"

"I know so. We haven't had one of those around these parts for a long time. It'll be a good time. We can barbecue, maybe hire a local band for some music, and have a good time with a bonfire and everything."

"I hope you're right." She bit the corner of her fingernail, a habit she'd never been able to break for long.

He took her fingers in his hand and kissed the tips. "Everything will be fine, baby. We will make this work."

"God I hope so, Caleb. This place means everything to me."

"I know it does. I'll be here as long as you want me."

His words brought her gaze to his. What she saw there took her breath away, but did she want to jump back into a long term relationship? Too many things were piling on top of her at the moment. Deciding on whether this was something she wanted for the rest of her life didn't have to be made right this minute.

They had a barn to raise.

"All right. Let's plan on this coming Saturday. Is that going to be enough time to bring in the troops? We are going to need a lot of people."

"No problem. I'll start making calls this afternoon. For now, let me get started on the old barn so we can at least have somewhere for the stallion and the gelding to be comfortable and a place to unload the mares when they arrive." He leaned down and brushed a kiss over her lips.

"I'm going to do some digging on the fracking stuff. I have a few contacts I can call to find out who owns the property and we need to figure out if they are doing anything illegal over there."

"Right. Good luck with your research and I'll see you at supper."

As he walked away, she drew on his strength and determination. Making everything work here was her only option. Running home to Daddy would make her a failure and failure wasn't in her vocabulary.

* * * *

A low misty fog rolled over the pasture early Saturday morning. The sun barely peeked over the horizon as trucks, cars, and wagons rolled into her yard. The wood needed for the barn had been delivered the day before and now sat in huge piles next to where the new barn would be erected. She'd given Caleb a blank check to buy what was needed since she didn't have really any clue how much of everything to buy.

Watching everyone pull in left her breathless. *So many people.* Caleb had called everyone he knew and they'd done the same. There were at least fifty people milling about waiting for direction on where to start.

"Attention everyone," Caleb shouted over the hum. "Pretty much everyone here knows me since I was born and raised here. This isn't for me. This is for my boss, Charlie Abrams." He held out his hand, bringing her up on the tailgate of his truck. "Charlie's barn caught fire earlier this week. The firemen did a fantastic job, but she still lost one of her client's horses."

The murmur through the crowd made her feel a little better. Everyone seemed as sad about it as she was. She raised her hand to silence the crowd. "I want to thank everyone for coming out this morning to help us put up a new barn. I'm in awe of you all."

"As long as there is beer and food, we're good. Good old barn raisin' is a fun time for all."

Charlie waved at the man in the back who'd spoken. He owned the feed store in town. "There is plenty of that and we even have a band coming this afternoon so this party can go on into the wee hours of the morning if you want it to."

"Then let's get to buildin'!"

Caleb whooped and hollered as he jumped down and held up his arms for her. He held her close until her feet hit the ground, sliding her all the way down his hard chest. "Damn you feel good."

"Later, handsome, and I'll make sure to thank you proper for all of this."

He gave her a quick kiss on the lips and headed off to supervise the building of the barn. She saw him stop and talk to someone she hadn't seen before. The guy had dark hair hidden beneath a straw cowboy hat. His height matched Caleb's and his build was similar with broad shoulders that stretched the t-shirt he was wearing. Caleb smiled over his shoulder at her and his friend's gaze fixed on her for a moment. She couldn't tell the color of his eyes, but he seemed to distance himself from those around him. *Maybe he needs some more friends.* He tipped his hat to her before Caleb corralled him and led him toward the construction zone. She would ask Caleb about him later.

The rest of the afternoon went by in a whirlwind of activity. The men worked on all the wooden beams, bolts, hammering, and sawing while the women handled the children and the food. People came in shifts to eat during the noon time while she grilled burgers, hot dogs, laid out a table with a ton of salads, and side items like potato salad and desserts. Beer flowed freely, but the guys were careful about drinking too much while they worked. Ladies gossiped around the shaded patio as the children ran around playing tag and swimming in the small pool she'd set up. Overall, she had to say it was a big success and by the time the sun started to set on the horizon, she had a new barn.

The band set up on her back lawn as music drifted over her where she sat with her back against Caleb's chest.

They'd taken ribbing all afternoon about their relationship. Several people had asked how long they had been dating while others gave her a dirty look. A few even kept themselves away from her. She just figured they were jealous of her relationship with Caleb.

His fingers trailed down her bare arm, bringing goose bumps to the surface. His touch always brought out the same responses in her and she loved how he made her feel so feminine. The scent of freshly washed man with a hint of a scent uniquely Caleb, made it to her nose and she took a deep breath to hold it inside her for longer. She loved the way he smelled.

One of his arms lay casually under her arm so his hand could lie touching her belly. He was talking to one of his buddies a few feet away, the rumble of his laughter, against her back.

They hadn't talked more about their relationship since her tantrum at the hospital. She needed to sit down with a glass of wine, him, a nice fire in the fireplace, or a cuddling spot out here without all these people around.

The bonfire they had going was fabulous. The band had people two-stepping to the beat of the music. Everyone seemed to be having a good time and the area around her heart warmed to having friends for a change. Caleb's friend she'd noticed earlier sat by himself on the bed of his truck dangling a beer from his fingertips. "Caleb? Who is the guy over there on the silver truck?"

"Chance Walker. He's a local guy who lives a few miles away. Runs some cattle on his place. He's a good guy although a bit quiet."

Her gaze swept over Chance noting how his eyes didn't seem to warm when they looked at people, a little mistrusting maybe. She would have to see what she could do to make him feel welcome in her home.

A cloud drifted across the moon, shadowing them briefly from its silvery light. Fireflies danced on the warm air in the distant pasture, making the night magical in its own way.

Caleb climbed to his feet and held out his hand. Without any words, he lifted her to her feet, and he led her toward the new barn. They hadn't had much time to talk during the day, but she'd felt his presence and his hot looks. Now would be a moment together.

When they crossed the threshold, he moved her into the shadows and pinned her against a new stall door. "How do you like your new barn?"

"It's fantastic. It's bigger and better than the old one. I can't thank you enough for arranging this."

He trailed a finger down her cheek before pushing his hand into her hair at the base of her neck. "It's what we do in Shadow. Friends help friends. Neighbors help neighbors. We all chip in when there is a need."

"I've never felt so accepted, well except for a few of the ladies who were giving me dirty looks whenever you touched me."

His tempting lips lifted in a smile. "There were a lot of men giving me those same looks whenever I got close to you, too. You are a gorgeous woman, Charlie, and I am honored to be with you."

She lifted up on her toes and brought her lips temptingly close to his. "It is I who is honored," she said in a whisper.

"I am a simple cowboy, Charlie. I live hard, play hard, and love harder. If that is enough for you, then I want to see where this might lead."

She pulled back a little so she could see his eyes. "What are you saying?"

"You might not want to hear this because I know you've been hurt in the past, but I love you and I want to spend the rest of my life making you feel that love with every breath I take."

Her heart hammered in her chest so hard, she thought it might burst right out from behind her rib cage. He loved her?

"It's okay if you can't say it back. I understand yo—"

She pressed her fingertips to his lips. "I love you too, Caleb, with everything inside me."

He nipped at the pads of her fingers before lowering her hand. "I promise to do my very best to make you happy."

"You already have."

With her hand in his, he walked them to the ladder leading up to the top of the barn. She hadn't noticed it before, but there was a flickering light up there that bounced shadows off the walls. Somehow, he'd managed to set up a beautiful scene just for her. Gauzy white material hung from the rafters, enveloping a small area in a glow of gold as the flicker from what looked like candles lit the enclosure.

"You didn't light real candles, did you?"

He choked on a laugh. "Candles in a barn is not a good idea. No, they are battery operated for effect."

She touched the material with her fingers, smiling as the silky stuff slid through.

Caleb touched her shoulder before turning her so she faced him. His hands slid into the hair at the base of her neck, removing the ponytail she'd placed there this morning. He smoothed back the wisps at her temples, tucking the hair behind her ear.

"I never thought I would fall in love. It was always a distant thing for me. I had too many other things in my life that were more important, or so I thought. You turned me inside out the moment I saw you standing in the pasture. You were so happy, you were laughing and all I could think about was having that excitement about life with me forever."

She ran her fingertips along his jawline. "You made me believe in love again. After everything I dealt with in my first marriage, I really never thought I would find someone who would be able to change my view on relationships. You have."

"You are my everything."

"Show me," she whispered against his mouth.

His eyes were bright with love and need, something she could totally relate to as he skimmed his hands down her shoulders to her fingers before bringing them to his mouth and kissing her palm. His lips lingered there for a moment before trailing kisses up the inside of her wrist, her elbow, her upper arm, and then her shoulder.

"You have such beautiful skin. I could nibble on this all day," he whispered near her ear before nipping at her earlobe.

Goose bumps exploded on her skin as she wrapped her arms around his waist and tipped her head to the side to give him better access. Her time with Caleb was special. Each and every time, he made love to her, she made new memories to replace the old ones.

His fingers inched up the edge of her tank top, baring her skin to his touch. Calluses abraded her abdomen as he moved around to her back and unlatched her bra. The moment his fingers moved along the underside of her breast, she moaned deep in her throat.

"I love you, baby, with everything that I am."

"I love you, too," she murmured, her gaze locked onto his as he stoked the fire to a blazing inferno of need.

He walked her backward until her knees hit the make shift bed of stacked hay bales. The whole set up was so Caleb, she couldn't help but smile.

"What?"

She shook her head. "A cowboy to the core."

A frown marred his gorgeous face until she smoothed it away with her fingers.

"I love that about you. This is you. Everything about this is you from the hay bales to the fairy lights. It's beautiful."

"I wanted something special for us when the craziness of the barn raising was done." He set her down on the bed and drew the tank top and bra off. "You have become my world. When I found you bleeding on the floor of the kitchen, I almost lost my mind. I am so sorry you thought I abandoned you at the hospital." He dropped down on his knees between her spread thighs. "I would never do anything to hurt you."

She pressed her fingertips to his lips to silence his words. "I overreacted and I'm sorry. I didn't know the barn was burning and the horses were in jeopardy. You rushed back here to save everything. I know that now."

Butterfly kisses ran across her cheeks. "It's over. You have a new barn and we have each other, that's all that counts." He laid her back on the blanket covered hay. "I'm going to make sweet love to you until you beg me to stop."

Her nipples pebbled into hard points as his mouth followed the waistband of her jeans. Her jeans parted as he unbuttoned them and pulled the zipper down one tooth at a time. Anticipation wracked her body, her breathing coming in rapid pants. Goose bumps ran across every inch of her skin as he slowly pulled her jeans off her hips and completely away from her body, leaving her underwear in place.

His wet tongue ran up the inside of her calf, around her knee, and then slipped up her inner thigh until he was so close to her pussy she could feel his hot breath against her center.

"Please, Caleb."

"I can smell your arousal."

The tip of his tongue skimmed over the crease between her thigh and her pussy. She shivered.

"Are you cold?"

"No, horny, yes."

He nipped at the skin of her inner thigh, dragging a small yelp and a deep groan from her lips. She felt his teeth grab the elastic of her underwear at her hip, pulling them down and off.

One finger slipped inside her. "Oh God."

"You are so wet, darlin'. I can't wait to be inside you."

"Hurry."

"Not yet, baby. There are things I want to do to you before we get to that part."

His tongue ran up one side of her slit and then the other, avoiding the part aching for him the most. Her clit felt hot and swollen. The throbbing in time with her heartbeat was disconcerting a little as she tried to wiggle to get him to lick her clit.

A sharp slap to her thigh made her moan deeper, the pain a piercing reminder not to move.

"I need you inside me."

His warm breath on her clit was a contrast to the cool slickness of his tongue. "Soon, baby, soon."

Two fingers penetrated her, pushing in and out in a steady rhythm meant to bring her to the peak. When his tongue finally began to flick quickly against her clit, her need shot to blinding in seconds.

She hovered on the brink, teetering on the edge of completion, needing just a tiny bit more pressure to send her over the edge.

The bastard slowed his assault, effectively bringing her down before she could come. *FUCK!* "You are a jerk, Caleb."

He chuckled lightly as he began again.

* * * *

Caleb was strung tighter than barbed wire around a fence pole. He wanted to be inside Charlie's warm pussy more than anything in the world, but he had a job to do as far as he was concerned. Her pleasure came before his and he would make damned sure her satisfaction was complete.

Her sweet scent met his nose as he ran his tongue over the hard nub of her clit. She tasted like heaven, all honeyed and warm just for him. Never in his life had he been with a woman like her. Strong, hardworking, loyal, special, ambitious, loving, and warm. All of these things were how he thought of her and now she was his to love until the end of time. How he'd come around to this, he wasn't sure, but here he was head over heels in love with this woman.

He nipped at the soft skin of her inner thighs, dragging a soft whimper from her lips.

Her clit stood out from its hood, all swollen and hot. He could tell she wanted to come very badly as she quivered under his touch. Her moans were like music to his ears, a soft melody of love.

She loved him.

He couldn't quite come to grips with that right at the moment, but it felt good, it felt right to be here with her.

"Caleb, please."

His cock ached behind the fly of his jeans. Soon, he would have to give into the desire to be inside her warmth, otherwise, he would come in his pants like a teenager.

It was time to give her an orgasm that would rock her world before he actually slid inside her and brought them both to sweet release.

He began a wicked rhythm of in and out with two fingers as he sucked on her clit softly at first and then harder. The moment he slid another finger into her ass, she screamed her release in a long wail of completion half the neighborhood probably heard. Good thing most of their guests had already left.

Sweat coated her body while she came down from her orgasm. The humidity of the night made him feel like he had a wet blanket over him, but he didn't care. He had the woman he loved beneath him.

He kissed his way from her hot center, over her abdomen, and stopped at the curve of her breast, raining small kisses down on the soft globe of flesh, leaving the nipple for last. The pink nub looked painfully tight and aroused, but he would get to it soon.

A soft nip to the underside of her breast had her hips shifting as if to find relief from the pressure building in her groin. He knew the feeling all too well. His cock ached with the need to be inside her.

She grasped at his shoulders, bringing him up her body until their lips met in a desperate kiss.

Her soft whimpers took him beyond control.

Kneeling between her thighs, he reached for the button on his jeans, but her hands stopped him. "Let me."

Within moments she had his pants down around his knees and her hand wrapped around his painful erection. "I can't. I'm about to blow, sweetheart."

"We have all night, right?"

"Yes, but I want to be inside you when I come."

"I need all of you." She ran a fingernail down his chest until she reached his cock. Her hand was tight and warm. "I want your cock in my mouth."

He closed his eyes as a shudder rolled through him. "Later. Tomorrow. Whenever you want, but right now I need you so bad, I have to feel your warmth around me."

A smile lifted the corners of her mouth as she guided him to her center. He slowly pushed until he was so deep, his balls were resting against her. Her eyes were bright with love and acceptance for the man he was. He knew right then that she was everything he needed. It felt like she had always been in his soul just waiting for him to find her. Now that he had, he would never let go.

Her arms wrapped around his shoulders and her lips found his as he slowly made love to her. Her mouth was heaven in its own right while he shifted his hips, driving his cock in and out of her pussy. *God, I love how she feels around me.* A moan escaped his lips only to be swallowed by her mouth.

"Harder," she whispered, wrapping her legs around his waist, and driving her heels into his buttocks.

The rhythm of his thrusts increased until he was slamming himself against her. She spread her thighs further, resting her heels on the bale of hay to anchor her butt for his hammering.

He couldn't hold on any longer. She was too wet, too sweet, and God help him, perfect.

The sensation shot up his spine from the base, forcing him to let go of his orgasm.

His shout of completion echoed off the rafters above him as she joined him with his name on her lips.

Chapter Fifteen

Sunrise spread it's warmth over them as it peeked over the horizon where they still lay snuggled on the makeshift bed in the hayloft.

Charlie lifted her head from Caleb's bare chest and moved so she could look into his face. His lashes still fanned across his cheeks while his eyes were closed in slumber. He held her close to his side even as he slept. He would be her protector for life.

Her thoughts turned to what she'd found out about the owner of the property housing the fracking machinery next door. It was a large co-op out of Dallas, but when she looked for more information it appeared to be a front for something. The building address didn't exist based on an internet search. The address was a vacant lot. While she dug further into the names of the corporation's governing board, she got more and more worried. It seemed that most of the information was buried. She couldn't find much at all.

Caleb's lips brushed against her forehead. "What are you thinking about so hard this morning?"

She ran her fingers over his chest, letting them tangle in the curls across the surface. "I hadn't had a chance to tell you what I'd found about our neighbors."

"And?"

"There isn't much to tell really. I think there might be something illegal going on over there, but I couldn't find much."

"Maybe you should let it alone for now."

She sat up, before brushing her hair off her shoulder. "I can't, Caleb. What if there are more explosions and more damage to my home because of what they are doing? I'm just not sure who to contact about it."

The crunch of gravel announced an early morning visitor. Sparky barked from the porch, the shrill sound proclaiming the visitor wasn't anyone they knew.

"Were you expecting someone?"

"No."

They both jumped up, rushing to get their clothes on so they could find out who was making such an early morning visit without an invitation.

A few moments later, they walked out of the big barn doors hand in hand to be faced with a nondescript black sedan parked in front of the house and two large men dressed all in black. Charlie glanced at Caleb before looking back at the men walking toward them. "Can I help you, gentlemen?"

"We are looking for Charlie Abrams."

"I'm her."

They looked at each other and then to Caleb. "Sir?"

"This is Charlene. She goes by Charlie. I am her foreman, Caleb. Is there something we can help you with?"

"Can we talk in private with you, ma'am?"

"Whatever you have to say you can say it in front of Caleb. He has as much at stake in this place as I do, and I don't keep secrets from him."

"All right, ma'am. We need to ask you to stop digging into the piece of property to your south."

"Why may I ask and while you're at it, who the hell are you to tell me what I can and cannot do?"

The man to the right reached into his breast pocket and held out a white business card. "We are with the FBI. We can't tell you much other than digging into information on what is going on over there could be detrimental to your health. We are currently investigating the activity going on over there, and we feel if you continue to dig, you will be putting our investigation in jeopardy."

She ran her finger over the edge of the card as she read the man's name. "Mr. Grassman. I would love to if you all are planning on making sure there are no more explosions on my property."

"Explosions?"

"Yes. There are been two so far and we aren't sure what it is all about. The first one broke several windows in my home and sent me to the hospital. My barn also caught fire and burned to the ground about a week ago, killing one of my client's horses. Obviously, this is something I need to worry about if my property and my animals are in jeopardy."

The two men looked at each other before focusing back on her. "We can't tell you any more than we already have, ma'am, but if I were you, I would be careful who you befriend and who you let on your property. There is a large investigation going on. Unfortunately, with you owning this property, you might be in the way so to speak."

"Great. Now I am a target too?"

"I can say yes or no to this." Mr. Grassman looked at Caleb with sharp eyes. "If you are a part of her life, you'll get her out of here to keep her safe."

Mr. Grassman nodded to his partner and they got back into their car.

Before Charlie could say anything more, they were nothing more than a cloud of dust down the driveway. "What the hell was that all about?"

"I'm not sure, baby, but I agree with the man. I think we need to keep you safe somehow. Can you go visit your dad for a while?"

"I'm not leaving, Caleb, no way. This place is my life. I'm not going away while someone else does the dirty work of rounding up these assholes."

"Don't do anything rash."

"I won't, but I'm not running either. We will hire more men to patrol the area so nothing happens if you want." She paced in front of him for several minutes, contemplating what could be done. "I'm buying a gun."

"What? Are you sure you need one?"

"I *am* buying a gun. My dad taught me how to shoot. I'm not a marksman by any means, but I can hit what I aim at and for my own peace of mind, I will have a firearm on me at all times." Her gaze locked with his before skimming down his chest, abdomen, and tight fitting jeans. "Well, maybe not always."

"We are in this together, Charlie. I will protect you with my life. I don't feel right about you having to carry a firearm."

She stood on her tiptoes, brushing her lips against his. "I love you. You know that. I feel the need to have one."

He shook his head at her stubbornness even as a smile lifted the corners of his mouth. "All right. We will go shopping for one this afternoon. In the meantime, keep your eyes and ears open."

"Yes, sir," she said with a saucy toss of her curls. When she glanced over her shoulder, giving him what she hoped was a sexy look, she squeaked and ran for the house as he growled behind her and gave chase.

The moment she cleared her bedroom doorway, he was on her like he would never let her go and she was definitely okay with that.

For now, they would let the mystery of their neighbors and their fracking be swept aside. She had a man she wanted to make love to and to see how far she could go before he lost control.

* * * *

Caleb was sleeping soundly in her bed as she snuck out the door of her room, trying to make as little noise as possible.

When she made it to her office, the light clicked on from the pressure of her fingers on the switch by the door. Something had been nudging at her brain all day and she had to figure out what it was.

Her computer desktop booted up as she settled into the chair behind her desk. She had to figure out what the connection of the drilling on the property next door had to do with her.

One of the articles that described fracking said it was a way for them to extract oil from areas that were difficult to drill before, by going down a mile or so and then drilling horizontally. If those people who owned the property next to hers were drilling horizontally onto her property, they were stealing oil and gas from her. If the process of fracking wasn't done properly, it could cause explosions, thus the blasts on her property.

She had to find out who was behind the things going on over there.

A click on the computer screen that talked about fracking gave her some information on how it all worked and a list of corporations that were registered with the EPA.

The sticky note next to her elbow contained the name of the corporation that held the deed on the property next to hers.

It didn't match to any of the names on the EPA's approved list.

So whoever owns the property over there is not approved by the EPA to do this type of drilling.

She glanced outside in the direction of the property where everything seemed to go on at all hours. Lights in the distance broke the darkness, making her wonder what went on over there during the night shift. Probably the same thing going on during the day, but it all seemed more covert at night.

The moon reflected a silvery light over her pasture as she stood at the window looking out. Pasture grass swayed slightly in the breeze that ruffled the curtains at the sides. Fireflies danced above the grass, flickering here and there for a short moment before disappearing into the darkness. A bird called to its friends in the night, but she was unsure of what kind it was. The sounds soothed her frazzled nerves, helping her think things through.

Her love for Caleb seemed endless and secure. She need not worry about how he felt now and even though they'd confessed their love for each other, she had to tell him every day so he never forgot. She remembered her father doing that with her mother throughout their marriage and when she asked him about it, he said he never wanted her to go to bed without knowing he loved her.

A strong pair of arms went around her waist, pulling her back against a wide chest.

"I missed you."

"Sorry. You were sleeping so soundly, I didn't want to wake you. Something about the drilling over there is making me crazy and I can't pinpoint it. I've read a lot of articles on it and tried tracking the corporation but usually comes up to a dead end."

His warm breath caressed her ear, sending shivers down her arms.

"We need to leave things to the FBI, baby. They are the professionals."

"I know, but it's hard for me to sit here and wait. I'm impatient."

A chuckle made his chest rumble against her back. "I hadn't noticed."

"What are you up to today?"

"I need to go over to Doc's and pick up the mares since the new barn is done. They can come home now where they belong."

"Thank you for setting that up."

"I'd do anything for you. I hope you know that."

"I do, Caleb, and I love you more every day."

His lips brushed along her neck, nipping as he moved along her shoulder blade. "What do you say we go upstairs and get naked?"

"Didn't we do that already?"

"Yes, but I want more. I will always want more where you are concerned." He glanced out the window before taking in their reflection again. "I have a better idea."

"Oh?"

"Yep." He lifted her pajama top over her head, revealing her breasts in the reflection of the window.

His hands ran over the globes, lifting and weighing them in his palms. One of his fingers went into his mouth to wet it and then circled her right nipple over and over. The flesh bunched tightly with his handling.

"I'm going to make you come so hard you see stars, right here in front of the window."

The thought of someone seeing them had her clit tingling. Unaware of her need for exhibitionism until now, she waited to see what he would do next.

One hand left her breast before skimming down her abdomen and disappearing inside her scrap of underwear if you could call it that since it didn't cover much. She'd bought some sexier under things online a few weeks ago, after the first time they'd had sex. The last thing she wanted was to be caught wearing granny panties in front of a new lover.

His finger glanced off her clit, drawing a small groan from her lips. He rubbed up one side and then the other, making her wet and wanting.

Her head fell back against his shoulder as she whimpered her need. "God Caleb. You drive me crazy wanting you inside me."

"Not yet, baby. I want the whole world to see you come against my hand."

When a finger slipped inside her, she spread her thighs wanting him deeper. He kissed down her spine, licking every little bump along the way until he reached her ass. A sharp nip on her butt cheek made her squeak before the pain morphed into something darker, something almost forbidden.

"Put your hands on the window and braced yourself." He instructed as he moved between her thighs. "Spread your legs wider."

Anticipating what he would do next, she held herself open for him, waiting for the brush of his tongue. God, she loved when he would eat her out.

The rough scrape of his tongue over her clit brought on a rush of wetness.

His soft moan vibrated against her pussy as he started licking her like a dying man.

When two fingers pushed up inside her, she almost lost all control. Her legs began to shake from the need to come. "Please Caleb."

"Not yet. Wait for it."

She tried focusing on anything but what he was doing. Training the stallion in the morning. Bringing the mares back from Doc's. The drilling on the other property. Her concentration narrowed a little until he nipped on her clit.

"Ah, God!" Her climax rose to sharpness, splashing over her like a massive wave until she felt lost and floating on the aftermath. Wetness coated her thighs as Caleb continued to softly lick her clit while she came down from her high.

Her legs gave out the moment he moved from between them, and she slid to the floor on the rug, her handprints leaving long wet streaks on the glass. Her breath rushed out between her lips while she tried to slow her heart rate. Her head hung low in the position she'd managed on her hands and knees.

Caleb leaned over her back, the hair on his naked chest tickling her. "Are you ready for me?"

"Always."

"Spread those thighs then, baby, I'm coming home."

The moment his cock pushed inside her, she moaned as her need exploded like a bottle rocket on the Fourth of July. His fullness stretched her with every stroke until he was deep enough she could feel his balls against her.

"Good God, you're perfect."

She smiled as she shifted to take him deeper. Every other lover had left her wanting in the end, but not Caleb. He made sure she'd been satisfied before he was.

A sharp tug on her hair made her realize he'd wrapped it in his fist as he started to thrust behind her. The pain on her scalp brought her need into a sharper focus while he pounded into her. His fingers bit into the skin at her hip, making her realize she would probably have a bruise there come morning, but she didn't care. Everything about Caleb's love making made her want him more.

This was love in the purest sense, something she'd never experienced before. He was her everything.

The hand on her hip moved around her front until he could reach her clit. Two sharp taps on the engorged little nub had her hovering on the verge of an orgasm. The second he pinched it between his first finger and his thumb, she shot off with a scream of his name as he growled hers into the base of her neck.

They collapsed to the floor in a heap of arms and legs, breathing hard, hearts racing, and fingers laced.

"I love you, Charlie."

"I love you, too," she whispered, bringing his hand to her mouth.

He pulled her back against his chest, slinging his leg over her thigh. "We should stay right here."

She laughed as she turned toward him so she could see his eyes. "You're crazy."

"Why?"

"One, this rug is not the softest thing to lay on. Two, there are no blankets or anything. Three, what if someone knocks on the door in the morning and we are still lying here naked as the day we were born?"

"You didn't seem to mind it when you thought someone might see you out the window."

"No one was out there." Her gaze shifted to the darkened window.

"How do you know? The light was on over there on the table, so we were illuminated in the window. If someone is out there, they would have been able to see everything from your bare breast in my hand to me fucking you from behind." His lips brushed her shoulder. "The guys working on the platforms on the other property could probably see us."

Goose bumps rose on her arms, before traveling over her torso. The thought of other men watching them, watching her, made her realize she was excited over the idea.

"I'm not into sharing, Charlie."

"I don't want to be shared."

"Good, but the idea of someone watching us excites you."

"Maybe. A little, I guess."

He ran a finger over her nipple where it was bunched tight. "More than a little, baby."

Her breathing has sped up just thinking about it. *This is wrong. Having sex with Caleb is one thing, but letting someone watch us? Nope. No way.* "I think we should take this into the bedroom."

"Do you want me inside you?"

Unable to deny that she wanted him, she nodded as he stood and held out his hand.

"Then I need to make sure my woman is taken care of."

They walked hand in hand down the hall to her bedroom, anticipation thick between them even though they'd just made love in the living room.

Once she crawled under the sheets with him next to her, she let him draw her into his embrace wanting his touch more than anything in the world. Eternity would never be enough with him, she realized as her lips met his.

His tongue touched her lips, slipping along the seam until she opened for him, letting him take control.

The moment his mouth left hers, she felt the slid of his lips along her jaw as she tipped her head to give him better access to her neck and shoulder.

Her eyes popped open as a loud whinny from out near the barn drifted through the open window in her room.

"Caleb?"

His head came up as he looked through the window. "The stallion. Something is wrong."

The shrill bark of his dog sounded muffled. He'd left Sparky on the porch.

He jumped up, grabbed his jeans and pulled them on. "Stay here."

"The hell you say. I am not staying here," she said, trying to find her jeans in the tangle of clothes on the floor.

"Charlie. I don't need to try to keep you safe as well as find out what is going on outside. Please, stay in the house."

"No. Those are my horses. I need to find out what is wrong," she said, slipping on her bra and a t-shirt.

"Damn stubborn woman," he grumbled. "Fine, but stay close."

The moment she had her boots and a light jacket, they moved toward the front door.

"Where are the rifle and pistol you purchased?"

"In the office. I'll get them."

Seconds later, she was back at his side with the rifle in one hand and the pistol in the other.

"Do you know how to use that?"

"Of course."

"Good. I'll take the rifle. You take the pistol. Do not leave my side unless I tell you to." He pulled open the door and they slipped outside onto the porch.

The stallion whinnied again, a sharp shrill sound, almost unnatural in its pitch. The shuffle of horses' hooves told her someone was in the barn who shouldn't be. The horses would not like someone they were not familiar with, especially the stallion.

"Follow close," Caleb whispered.

She nodded, holding onto his belt loop.

They reached the barn doors and he looked around the edge of the sliding door before moving into the interior. Shadows stretched across the floor from the moon shining in the big bay doors. Another whinny echoed in the space, raising the hair on her arms. Hooves hit the back of the stall.

There was someone in the stallion's stall.

Chapter Sixteen

A shot rang out right before Caleb felt the hot fire of a bullet grazing his arm. He grabbed Charlie and shoved her down inside the stall they were standing in front of seconds before another bullet slammed into his gut.

Fucking son of a bitch!

His hand came away covered in blood and he sank to the floor.

"Oh my God! Caleb? You're bleeding."

"Ssh. For God's sake, be quiet," he whispered as he crawled behind the door.

She stripped off her jacket and held it against his wound.

"Where's your gun?"

"Right here, but never mind that. We have to call an ambulance."

Her eyes got huge when they heard a voice call out. "Charlie, come out here in the middle where I can see you."

He held up his fingers to her lips to make her stay quiet.

"I know you're in there. Get out here now!"

Terror held her tongue as they waited for several seconds. The voice was familiar, but in his foggy brain, he couldn't place it.

"If you don't come out here, I will come in there after you and I will shoot your lover right between the eyes while you watch."

"Caleb?" she mouthed, her hand clutching at the pistol. He moved closer to his ear so he could hear her. "It's Aaron."

Now he knew why the voice was familiar. *I'm going to kill that motherfucker.* "Put it in your pocket so he can't see it."

Her body shook as she touched his shoulder. "I love you. Don't do anything heroic. Stay here. I will deal with Aaron."

"I love you, Charlie, but don't try to take him on by yourself."

"He wants me alive so he can take me with him. I will use that to my advantage." She climbed to her feet, hiding the pistol in her pocket. Luckily, it was a fairly small pistol.

She moved out of the stall and into the dirt walkway. He wished the lights were on so he could see what was going on. His chest hurt knowing she was in danger. Keeping her alive and getting out of this situation was his goal.

His head felt groggy, making it difficult to focus on anything. He heard Sparky barking, scratching, and growling, but he wasn't sure from where. *The tack room?*

"Charlie, Charlie, Charlie."

"What do you want, Aaron?"

"You know what I want, sweetheart. I want you no matter what it takes."

"I am not going anywhere with you. This is my home and these horses are my life."

Caleb could hear the shuffle of feet. He rolled over on his side, shaking his head to clear his vision. Charlie had moved a little closer to Aaron. *Don't do it! Don't get too close!*

Aaron laughed a deep throaty chuckle that made him sound all the more crazy. "It doesn't matter what you want.

It only matters what I want." Aaron shuffled a little to the side before turning toward her again. "You see, you are the woman I crave. Nothing else matters. Not this property. Not the drilling. Nothing."

"Drilling?"

"You never knew, but the property next door belongs to me lock, stock, and barrel. We've been drilling for months sideways onto your property to take out the oil that the surveyors found right before you bought it. If the people who owned it before would have known, they would never have lost it to the bank. The oil deposits are huge."

"You fucking asshole! I almost lost my life because your people caused an explosion that took out my windows."

He shook his head. "My poor Charlie. So worried about whatever she sees right in front of her. Don't you see? I'll be a very rich man, richer than I am now, and you'll be by my side."

"I don't love you, Aaron."

"Love?" His laughter turned maniacal as he moved toward the gun she now saw lying on the bale of hay near the wall. "Love doesn't have a damn thing to do with it. You are a possession to me, Charlie, nothing more and I always get what I want." He turned back toward her, waving a pistol like a flag.

He reached for her arm just as she pulled out her own gun. "Don't touch me."

"Do you really think you can shoot me?"

"You shot Caleb. It is self-defense."

"I have more attorney's in my pocket than you have money. Whatever charges you think you can come up with wouldn't stick, and you know it."

"Attempted murder comes to mind."

"I have an alibi. I was in Dallas tonight."

Caleb looked down at the blood seeping between his fingers. If he didn't get help soon, there would be no future for him and Charlie.

Aaron lunged and the pistol went off. His body jerked as surprise registered on his face and he slowly sank to the floor beneath him, his eyes fixed in a lifeless stare.

"Charlie?"

"I'm fine, Caleb."

"Thank God, but, baby, you need to call an ambulance like right now." He slid down until he was lying flat on the floor and lost consciousness, his last thought of how much he loved her and wanted to see what life would be like with her by his side.

* * * *

Charlie rubbed her arms to calm the chill bumps running up and down them as she paced the waiting room at the hospital. They wouldn't let her in the back because she wasn't family. *What the hell? I'm as close as family.*

A man approached the waiting room desk, his wheat colored hair glinting red in the overhead lights. He was tall and broad shouldered and his stance reminded her of Caleb.

"My name is Cameron Armstrong. Caleb Armstrong is my brother. I need to see him."

"Just one moment. I will call the nurse." The woman picked up the phone, talked for a few moments, and then hung up. "They will be out to get you in a minute."

Charlie took a deep breath. "Cameron?"

He turned toward her and she could see the resemblance in Cameron's facial features. "Yes?"

"I'm Charlie Abrams."

"Oh, I see."

"I know I'm probably not on your priority list as Caleb's employer, but they won't let me back there and I'm going a little crazy right now. If you could, please come out and let me know what's going on?"

Cameron put his hands on her shoulders. "I will let you know as soon as I can and I know all about you and Caleb, so you are more important to my brother than you realize. He loves you from what I've heard, and my brother doesn't fall in love easily." He leaned down and pulled her into a hug. "Chin up. He'll be fine. He's too stubborn to be down for long."

"Thanks," she whispered, holding back a tear that threatened to escape.

"Do me a favor and watch for a harried looking couple who will be rushing through here in a few moments. Our parents are on the way."

"Of course."

"I'll be back in a few minutes." He rubbed her arms for a second, but when the door to the back opened and a nurse poked her head out, he disappeared through it in a rush.

Charlie chewed her fingernail on her right thumb while she paced the floor in front of the door. She wanted to be ready the moment they came out and told her anything. Caleb was her life, and she wasn't about to let him go anytime soon.

She took a seat on one of the hard white plastic chairs facing the door. Her hands were pinned between her knees as she rocked back and forth trying not to picture her life without Caleb. He'd come into her life like a hurricane, blowing in on a rush, making her feel things she hadn't wanted to feel until he'd swept her up, held her close, and made her realize he was everything she needed in a man. Without him next to her, she'd survive, but she would be miserable and lonely because putting someone in his place wasn't something she wanted to contemplate.

The door opened to the outside a few moments later as a frantic couple rushed in.

"We are Caleb Armstrong's parents. We need to see him."

"One moment please." The attendant picked up the phone again and within a few seconds, Cameron came out to take his mother's hand.

"Let me talk to Charlie a minute and we'll go back." Cameron sat down on the seat next to her, taking her hands in his. "He is in surgery. The bullet was lodged near his spine and they are doing everything they can to get it without damaging something in the process."

Her heart dropped into her stomach as tears filled her eyes and began to run down her face. "Did he regain consciousness at all?"

"No. They took him right in. He'd bled so much they were worried they couldn't stabilize him."

"Oh God, Cameron. I can't lose him."

"I know. Prayers are good." He squeezed her fingers and motioned for his parents to join them. "Mom. Dad. This is Charlie. She is Caleb's girlfriend."

His parents glanced at each other before his mother came forward and drew her up for a hug. "He'll be okay. Let's pray together and then we will sit here until we hear something."

The four of them joined hands as his father led them in prayer. She felt every bit of energy they brought with them run through their hands into her body. God was with him in that operating room, this she knew, and He would watch over him until they could be together again.

Several hours went by while they sat in the waiting room. She feared the news wouldn't be good the longer they waited. The hand on the clock seemed to stall, but then the next moment it sped by.

Cameron got them all coffee, something strong to keep her awake.

She wanted to ask Cameron questions about Caleb's childhood, things she didn't know about him like what was he like as a boy? Did he have a lot of girlfriends in high school? Did he play sports? Was he a book nerd burying himself in stories? Did he always want to be a cowboy? She couldn't hold back the tears as she dabbed at her eyes and blew her nose.

Cameron sat next to her and put his arm around her shoulders. "He'll be okay."

"How do you know?"

"Because I know my brother. He's stubborn and when he has something special like you to live for, he won't give up."

"God, I hope so."

"They'll bring us news soon."

She nodded, terrified that the news would be bad when they did bring it.

A doctor in blue scrubs came around the corner, his head covered in a short blue cap tied in the back and his shoes encased in stretchy things. "Mr. and Mrs. Armstrong?"

Caleb's parents rose from their seats in the corner. "Yes?"

"I'm Doctor Loveless. I am the surgeon who treated Caleb."

"Is he okay, Doctor?"

"Yes. He came through the surgery fine. We got the bullet out, but at this point, we aren't sure if there is damage to his spinal cord. The bullet was lodged next to it. He had some damage to his internal organs, but we managed to control the bleeding and he'll be fine with that area."

"What does that mean?"

"He might not have use of his legs."

"Oh God." His mother sank down on the seat, pressing her tissue to her lips.

"When will you know?" his father asked.

"In a few days. There is inflammation. Right now we aren't sure. It's promising that everything will be fine, but I don't want to get your hopes up. I'll be checking on him regularly over the next few hours."

Cameron spoke up as he put his arm around her shoulders. "Can we see him?"

"In a little while. I want him to get out of recovery and into his room before you go in there. He might sleep for several hours before he opens his eyes."

"Thank you, Doctor Loveless. We appreciate you working on our boy."

"My pleasure."

Charlie stood there in shock. She wasn't sure what to think. *He might not walk again?*

"Look at me, Charlie. You have to be strong for him. If he indeed loses the use of his legs, it doesn't change how you feel about him, right?"

"Of course not. I love him."

"Then you have to make sure he doesn't do the pity party thing because you know he will. He will try to shove you away for your own good. You can't let him do that. For now, let's take this one day at a time, shall we?"

She nodded and walked into his embrace. Funny, she'd only just met him, but she felt closer to him than any other person on earth except Caleb. The brother she'd never had.

A nurse came out to find them two hours later. "Are you with Caleb Armstrong?"

His brother got up and moved toward her. "Yes. These are his parents, I'm his brother, and this is his girlfriend."

"You can see him now. He's in his room on the surgical recovery floor in room 341. He is not alert yet, but he's awake."

Her heart raced as they walked to the elevator and rode up to the third floor. Her palms were sweaty as she waited to see him.

When they walked into the room, she stopped breathing for a moment while she waited for him to breathe. His chest rose and fell, making her feel better. The monitor over his head bleeped in a rhythmic pattern with his heart beat.

She let his parents move to his left side and take his hand. His mother spoke in whispers next to his ear, so she couldn't hear what she said.

Caleb didn't move.

If the monitor continued to beep, she would be okay.

After a few moments, she moved to his right side and reached over the railing to touch him. His skin was warm, thank goodness. When she picked up his hand and laced her fingers with his, she gently squeezed his hand. "Caleb. I'm right here. I'm not leaving until you wake up and smile at me." She took a deep breath. "Your parents are here too, and Cameron as well. You are in good hands. Doctor Loveless said you did well in surgery, but we have to wait for you to wake up." A tear slid down her cheek. "I love you," she whispered before she brushed her lips against his.

"I love you too," he murmured even though he didn't open his eyes. "Stay with me." He squeezed her fingers.

Unable to believe he spoke, she looked at his face. He looked like he was still asleep, but she could tell his breathing had changed a little and when she glanced at the monitor, his heart beat a bit faster.

Cameron slid a chair up so she could sit and hold his hand.

"We are going to go down and get some food. Do you want us to bring you something?" Cameron asked. "You need to eat to keep your strength up."

"No, I'm fine."

"I'll bring you a sandwich anyway."

She smiled as they walked out of the room, leaving her to spend time with Caleb alone. Trailing her fingertips over his hand, she started talking, telling him about her childhood, her parents, and her plans for the ranch. Her future included him on every level and it was important that he knew that.

His family brought her some food, which she ate but didn't taste.

The hours went by without her moving at all. She wouldn't leave his side even to pee.

Sometime during the night, she'd fallen asleep with her head on his bed next to his hip. His parents had taken a hotel room not far from the hospital so they could be close, and Cameron had taken up residence in the waiting room crammed into a chair.

The moment she felt his hand in her hair, she sat bolt upright. "You're awake. Oh, thank you, God." She touched his face. "Are you in pain?"

"Yes."

"I'll get the nurse—"

"No, not yet. I need to see you first." He reached up, running his fingers over her lips. "I didn't imagine you."

"I'm right here."

"I love you, Charlie."

"I love you too. I'm so sorry you were shot. If I would have known Aaron was that crazy, I would have done something to keep you safe."

"Baby, it's okay." He frowned. "What happened? I don't remember much."

"What do you remember?"

His forehead crinkled as he tried to think. "The pain in my gut and you standing in the middle of the barn talking to him. He said he was going to take you away."

"Not much after that other than he made a grab for me and I shot him."

"Where is he now?"

"Shadows Funeral Home, I guess. That's who picked up the body after the police did their thing." She tapped her fingers to her lips. "Which reminds me, I need to call them now that you are awake. They need a statement from you when you can so they don't arrest me."

"Arrest you? It was self-defense, baby. They can't arrest you."

"It's a formality, Caleb. Don't worry. They found his gun and are working on matching the bullet to the one the doctor took out of you."

His eyes began to droop.

"You need to sleep to get better."

"I need to rest a little and then we can talk more."

"I'm not going anywhere. I'll be right here when you wake up." A soft snore met her ears a few minutes later, bringing a smile to her lips as she whispered, "I love you."

* * * *

Caleb held his breath when the doctor ran the end of his instrument down the bottom of his foot. He'd been able to move his legs a little in the bed for the last two days while he recovered in the hospital, but he was disappointed he couldn't do more.

"Can you feel that?"

"Yes."

Charlie sighed beside him as she gripped his hand.

"It is sharp or dull?"

"Sharp."

Doctor Loveless smiled. "I think you'll make a full recovery, Caleb. You'll need physical therapy, of course, to regain your full mobility, but it appears the damage to your spinal cord is minimal."

"So I'll be able to walk?"

"Yes. It will take time and you don't need to overdo."

He smiled finally thinking it was going to be okay. "Thanks, Doc."

"My pleasure. I will release you tomorrow after we set up everything. You'll need to keep doing the dressing changes on your abdomen and I'll see you in two weeks to take those staples out."

"I'll see you then."

After Doctor Loveless walked out, he grabbed Charlie and brought her down for a kiss. "I love you, baby."

"I love you too. I'm so glad you'll be coming home tomorrow."

"Are you sure you want me to come to the ranch? I can go to my parents' place for a few days and—"

"Not on your life. You're coming home with me. I need you next to me when we sleep at night, and I want to wake up to your face in the morning."

"I'll need care over the next couple of weeks, you won't be able to do and run the ranch at the same time."

"I'll hire someone to help me and with Amy there, we'll be fine."

"Did the mares get moved back? And what about Sparky? He was locked in the tack room, I think, when the whole thing went down."

"Sparky is fine. I let him out after the ambulance left with you and yes, Doc Milburn brought the mares over for me when he heard about your accident. He got them all situated and has been helping Amy care for them for the last few days. I owe him a lot."

"We do."

His parents and Cameron walked in a few moments later, clearing their throats while he thoroughly kissed his woman. "What?"

"I see you're feeling better," Cameron stated as he took a seat in the corner. "Ready to go home?"

"Doctor said tomorrow."

"How did the test come out?"

"Good. I could feel everything I was supposed to. With some therapy, I should be good as new soon."

"That's wonderful, Caleb," his father responded. "We can't wait to see you up and about again."

His parents glanced at each other with secretive little smiles. "What's going on?"

"Nothing really. We are just wondering when you and Charlie are going to make things official?"

"Mom, don't start thinking about weddings. Charlie and I are new at this couple thing. It might be a while before you can talk to her about a wedding." He touched Charlie's cheek. "We'll get there soon enough."

Charlie gave him a blinding smile and all was right in his world.

Epilogue

Spring arrived in Shadow, bringing the blooming flowers, warmer days, and longer nights.

Charlie held her breath as she watched the mare in her stall struggling with the birth of their first foal on the ranch. Caleb stood by her side, strong, and healthy.

"Soon, baby."

"I know. I'm just excited. This is our first baby on the place."

"Yeah."

"We've done well over the past year." She glanced up into his eyes. "Wow. It's been a full year since I got here and you found me spinning around in circles in the overgrown pasture like some silly little girl."

He kissed her nose. "You were gorgeous even then. I fell in love with that silly little girl."

Her hand rested on her still flat abdomen. "And now, we are making our own little girl."

"Or boy."

She laughed as she leaned into his embrace. "Or boy just like his daddy with a killer smile and a heart of gold."

"We still need to plan the wedding and we'd better make it soon since we've gone and done things a little backward."

"A small ceremony will be fine. Our parents, your brother, and a few friends are all we need."

"I agree. I think right here in the barn would be nice."

"Me too." She turned in his arms and looped hers around his shoulders. "How about a month from today. I won't be showing yet since we are only eight weeks along, and we can have a barbecue or something."

"I like the way you think, my love."

"Good. I'll call your mother and mine. We'll get together Saturday and start planning. Besides, it will be a good idea to get the two of them together since they haven't met yet."

"And I can take the two dad's out for a beer or two."

She brushed her lips against his. "I love you, Caleb. You are everything I could have wished for in the man I fell in love with."

"I love you too, baby."

After a very thorough, panty-melting kiss, she leaned back and looked into his eyes. "Race you to the bed!"

The End

About the Author

Sandy Sullivan is a romance author, who, when not writing, spends her time with her husband Shaun on their farm in middle Tennessee. She loves to ride her horses, play with their dogs and relax on the porch, enjoying the rolling hills of her home south of Nashville. Country music is a passion of hers and she loves to listen to it while she writes.

She is an avid reader of romance novels and enjoys reading Nora Roberts, Jude Deveraux and Susan Wiggs. Finding new authors and delving into something different helps feed the need for literature. A registered nurse by education, she loves to help people and spread the enjoyment of romance to those around her with her novels. She loves cowboys so you'll find many of her novels have sexy men in tight jeans and cowboy boots.

Sandy's website
www.romancestorytime.com

Other books by Sandy

Love Me Once, Love Me Twice (Montana Cowboys 1)
Before the Night is Over (Montana Cowboys 2)
Two for the Price of One (Montana Cowboys 3)
Difficult Choices (Montana Cowboys 4)
Doctor Me Up (Montana Cowboys 5)
Stakin' His Claim

Country Minded Cougar
Meet Me in the Barn
Taming the Cougar
Trouble With a Cowboy
Gotta Love a Cowboy
Make Mine a Cowboy (Cowboy Dreamin' 1)
Healing a Cowboy's Heart (Cowboy Dreamin' 2)
For the Love of a Cowboy (Cowboy Dreamin' 3)
Tempted by the Cowboy (Cowboy Dreamin' 4)
Forever Kind of Cowboy (Cowboy Dreamin' 5)
Kiss Me, Cowboy (Cowboy Dreamin' 6)
A Cowboy and a Country Song (Cowboy Dreamin' 7)
A Cowboy of My Own (Cowboy Dreamin' 8)
A Cowboy's Promise (Cowboy Dreamin' 9)
Falling Hard (Eight Second Ride Book 1)
Loving Hard (Eight Second Ride Book 2)
SEALed by Love (Omega Team Kindle World)
Lost Soul (Lone Star Burn Kindle World)